Christmas Wishes

SEVEN TINE
RANCH

CARMEN PEONE

A Novella

IRON
STREAM
FICTION

BIRMINGHAM, ALABAMA

Christmas Wishes

Iron Stream Fiction
An imprint of Iron Stream Media
100 Missionary Ridge
Birmingham, AL 35242
IronStreamMedia.com

Library of Congress Control Number: 2025946141

Scriptures taken from the Holy Bible, New International Version®, NIV®. Copyright © 1973, 1978, 1984, 2011 by Biblica, Inc.™ Used by permission of Zondervan. All rights reserved worldwide. www.zondervan.com. The "NIV" and "New International Version" are trademarks registered in the United States Patent and Trademark Office by Biblica, Inc.™

Cover design by For the Muse Designs

ISBN: 978-1-56309-799-7 (paperback)
ISBN: 978-1-56309-800-0 (eBook)

1 2 3 4 5—29 28 27 26 25

"If you love stories brimming with connection, family, and wishes coming true, be sure to read *Christmas Wishes*. It's a wonderful recipe for a heartwarming holiday read."

—**Shanna Hatfield**, USA Today best-selling author

"Heartfelt, immersive, and deeply relatable—Carmen delivers a Christmas romance full of love, dreams, and tender sacrifices."

—**Milla Holt**, author of *Old Town Symphony*

"*Christmas Wishes* is a fast-paced, fun story of romance, Christmas, and miracles."

—**Heidi M. Thomas**, award-winning author of *Rescuing Hope*

"This story of love, sacrifice, and selflessness at the Seven Tine Guest Ranch can only be told this powerfully through the skill and caring heart of Carmen Peone. The deep faith and spirit of these memorable characters are not only unforgettable but also inspiring."

—**K. S. Jones**, award-winning author of *Tastefully Texas*, book one in the True Hearts of Texas series

"A warm Christmas tale of hopes and dreams amid obstacles and challenges. And the welcome message that trust and love come from a willing and honest heart."

—**Michelle Ferrer**, award-winning author of Western stories

"Author Carmen Peone has crafted a compelling Western romance story. *Christmas Wishes*, part of the Seven Tine Guest Ranch series, is inspired by Carmen's experience living, working, and riding horses on the Colville Indian Reservation in Eastern Washington. When the first chapter pulls you in as it did with me, relax and enjoy the read!"

—**Joyce B. Lohse**, award-winning author of Now You Know Bios and Western history

"*Christmas Wishes* is the perfect addition to Carmen Peone's Seven Tine Ranch series. Known for wrangling tough topics, Peone delivers a page-turner that's wrapped in the sweetest holiday romance. Mandie and Hudson must learn the art of compromise as they navigate the difficult choices so many couples face, particularly sacrificing personal ambition to maintain cultural tradition and build a life together. If you love holiday stories filled with faith, family, and heart, you'll love *Christmas Wishes*."

—**Charlsie Estess**, author of *When the Ocean Roars*

"What makes a Christmas book even better? How about a wedding or two thrown in there? *Christmas Wishes* has that and more. Carmen Peone brings the holidays to life as Mandie tackles wedding planning for Seven Tine Ranch. Those familiar with the Seven Tine Ranch crew will enjoy catching up with some familiar faces. And those new to the family will want to learn more about the people in Mandie's and Hudson's lives. Either way, this book will boost your Christmas spirit and have you hanging on for a happy ending."

—**Suzie Waltner**, author of the Love in Color series

With God all things are possible.

—Matthew 19:26

CHAPTER 1

M andie had to get out of the stifling kitchen—for good. The Christmas music drifting from her cell phone was the only thing keeping her in the holiday mood. She turned the sizzling rib eye steaks with metal tongs on the commercial grill, stirred the barbecue beans, and tossed the salad.

"How are those potatoes looking?" Mandie asked Shirley Scott, the sixty-something, well-rounded, full-time cook who assisted her at Seven Tine Guest Ranch. Mandie had to smile at Shirley's colorful Christmas stocking apron. It helped to brighten her sour mood.

Shirley opened the oven and poked the potatoes with a fork. "They're about done. Give them, say, ten more minutes." She closed the door.

Mandie wiped the sweat off her brow with a kitchen towel, tossed it over her shoulder, and pulled up the sleeves of her red elf Christmas sweater. A favorite in her collection of twenty-five—one for each day leading up to her favorite holiday.

"So, you gonna talk with Syd today?" Shirley crossed the linoleum floor and set the fork on the counter.

"That's the plan." As long as God gave her the courage to approach her boss and longtime friend about taking over as the official guest ranch event planner.

Sydney Moomaw Hardy had enough on her plate. She was the CEO of the ranch, was a *New York Times* best-selling author, was on the road much of the time giving speeches at women and ranch conventions, and had a possible movie option from her autobiography. At least that was Mandie's take on things.

"I have to have a solid future for Nona." Her precious five-year-old daughter. "Event planning has to be more secure than being a cook. No offense."

"None taken."

"Especially when there's no guarantee a man will hang around long enough to take care of us." In her head, Mandie knew Hudson would never abandon her like the other men in her life had. If only her heart would keep up, leaving her the strength to shove the triggers away.

Shirley went back to the worktable, picked up a spatula, and waved it around. "I hear ya. I'm fortunate God blessed me with my man. He can be ornery at times, but he's mostly fun and loving."

Mandie longed for years of bliss like Shirley and her husband had. "How are the apple pies coming along?" The song changed to "O Holy Night." To go with the holiday music, the kitchen needed more Christmas decorations. The pint-sized nativity on the counter wasn't cutting it.

Shirley held her hand over one of the pies on the wooden counter of the worktable. "They're golden brown and still warm."

Mandie took a deep breath. Cinnamon and nutmeg tickled her senses as they rushed up her nostrils.

"How many guests are eating tonight?" Mandie fetched a large bowl of green salad and a variety of dressings from the commercial refrigerator and set them on a metal roller cart.

"Fourteen. Most of them are big, hungry men too."

Sweat ran down Mandie's temples as she continued to flip the steaks. Her tummy grumbled. She couldn't wait to sink her teeth into a juicy rib eye.

"They picked a great week to come for a retreat." All attorneys from a big firm in Tacoma. Good thing there were only a few inches of snow on the early December ground.

Mandie downed the last of her tepid candy cane–laced hot chocolate and clinked the mug in the sink. She'd always had the desire to do more than cook. Yeah, she was an efficient ranch cook, but she wanted to expand her horizons and use her God-given talents to plan events like anniversary parties and weddings. Ceremonies where new love tangles with music and vows to protect, and long-standing commitments to offer reminders that love can endure tough times.

She wanted out of the hot, confining kitchen to spread her wings.

There was so much more in her. She imagined herself navigating music, flowers, meals, and guest lists. Most importantly, she wanted to show her daughter that women can reach their heart's desires and not be stuck in a box.

The batwing doors flew open, and Sydney, sporting her four-month pregnancy mound and a messy updo, breezed through. "It smells delightful in here, ladies. Is dinner almost ready? I know the guests are." She chuckled. "They're out there salivating."

"Give us five more minutes." Mandie's tummy twisted at the thought of approaching Sydney about event planning. "I need to talk to you about something." She brushed a stray strand of damp hair out of her face and tucked it behind her ear.

"I have a bit of time after dinner." Sydney crossed the kitchen, opened a cupboard door, pulled down a box of crackers, and slipped a bite into her mouth.

"How are you feeling?" Mandie asked.

"Not too bad. I'm a little queasy. But I think I might just need something to eat." Sydney patted her protruding tummy.

"Well, we got apple pie made especially for baby girl." Mandie motioned to Sydney's belly with a nod and a smile. They all hoped for a girl, anyway.

"I'm sure she'll enjoy it. As for me . . ." Sydney held up the crackers and whisked out of the kitchen.

"I hated morning sickness." Shirley took the potatoes out of the oven and set them on the wooden counter that spanned the wall between the two sets of batwing doors.

"Thank goodness it's not as bad as it was with Lester. Poor thing." Mandie recalled all the sick days Sydney had when she was carrying her son.

"Especially with a rambunctious two-year-old in tow." With metal tongs, Shirley pointed to Trey and Sydney's family photo hanging above her.

Mandie plated the steaks and added a green garnish. After Shirley transferred the baked potatoes into a bowl, poured the barbecue beans into another one, and gave the salad a good tossing, dinner was ready. Mandie and Shirley set the rest of the food on the cart and rolled it into the Seven Tine dining area. Outside the sixteen-thousand-square-foot log lodge's big, bay windows, floodlights revealed snow falling like powdered sugar.

"That smells heavenly," a female guest said as she took off her red reading glasses.

"Can't wait to sink my teeth into those steaks." One of the male guests wearing a Seattle Seahawks sweatshirt rubbed his hands together.

Mandie and Shirley laid out the food on a long, Christmas-themed table and went back into the kitchen to retrieve decanters of hot cider.

When an icy wind and a dusting of snow blew in, Mandie lifted her chin to see her fiancé, Hudson Piccolo, in the foyer, shedding his coat. He wore cowboy boots and jeans along with his tan jacket, dark-brown Stetson, and deerskin gloves.

She loved how his short sandy-brown sideburns flared from his cowboy hat.

He caught her eye, smiled, and strode into the great room. Mandie met him at the entrance where a decorated and lit Christmas tree stood guard.

The whole interior of the lodge and gift shop resembled a Hallmark Christmas movie. Lighted garlands with red-and-white silk poinsettias ran up both handrails of the staircases that straddled the great room, curled around the wagon wheel chandeliers, and stretched across the blazing floor-to-ceiling rock hearth. Trey had put a stop to Mandie decorating the stuffed elk head over the fireplace and the other deer and moose mounted on the walls.

She snorted. *Fun police.*

Mandie returned the smile. "Why don't you grab some dinner?" She motioned to a table boasting a three-tiered glass candleholder with lit vanilla pillars encircled by a snippet of pine in the center.

"I have some exciting news." Hudson's sea-blue eyes lit up.

Oh, that makes two of us. "Perfect. Let me see if I can catch up with Sydney for a quick minute, then I'll join you for dinner."

He bent his five-eleven frame over and drew her in for a hug. He seemed a little more jittery than usual, which probably stemmed from his caffeine addiction.

Several inches shorter than him, Mandie rose on her tiptoes and kissed his cold cheek. While Hudson took a seat, Mandie approached the office perched under the north staircase. Voices crept through the cracked door.

"What are you gonna do?" Trey Hardy asked his wife, Sydney.

"This is too much," Glenda, Sydney's sister and Seven Tine bookkeeper, said. "It's too close to Christmas."

"I can't say no," Sydney said. "I can't tell these people, 'I'm sorry. You can't have your wedding here. Sorry the pipes froze and burst in your venue. Sorry all your flowers and decorations were trashed. Life sucks.'"

"With Robert and Chad and their families coming in," Trey said, "we just don't have the time or the space."

"We're going to have to *make* time. And space. Let's give them a little Christmas magic. Yeah?" Sydney sounded more stressed than normal.

"I don't know," Trey said. "We have to head out to pick Leena up from the airport."

Oh, c'mon, Trey. Mandie shook her head. *The Spokane airport is only a couple hours away. No big deal.*

Sydney had a joy-filled snap to her voice. "I'll pick her up."

"I can pick our daughter up." Trey's voice held a guilt-ridden tone.

"You have that photo shoot in the morning. There's no way you can pick her up and get back in time."

"I'll see if I can move the shoot." A pause. "Hey, how's it going?" Another pause. "I'm wondering if we can reschedule the photo shoot."

Come on, Janet. Say yes. Mandie bit her bottom lip.

"No? Okay. I understand. See you tomorrow then."

Mandie rested her palm on the base of her neck. This was her chance. She could do it. She could help. After she lightly knocked on the door, she pushed it open.

From the comfort of a wingback chair in front of the office desk, Sydney set a Sprite on the coffee table and watched Mandie enter the room. "Sorry. I can't talk right now." She blew out a deep breath.

From the desk chair and wearing a frown, Glenda pinned a pay-attention gaze on Mandie, shook her head, then nodded at Sydney.

Mandie ignored her warning to leave Sydney alone. She wasn't about to give up her chance to help and have her talents seen. "I-uh . . . heard your dilemma. I wasn't eavesdropping. I just walked up on it."

"And?" Trey arched his brows. Slim but muscular, he towered over her.

"You know, I've been wanting to help with event planning—"

"We need you in the kitchen." Sydney shook her head. "You know how to run it with your eyes closed. I can't afford to give you up where we need you the most."

Mandie put up a finger. "Hear me out."

"Fine." Sydney reached for another cracker. "What's your plan?" She took a bite.

"I have an entire book filled with ideas and notes. And, c'mon, I've already been planning my New Year's Eve wedding. I can plan this one too. It'll go with the flow. I can do this. I'm already in wedding mode. Let me help. You've got your hands full with the book tours, the ranch conferences, your speaking engagements, kids." Mandie added flair to her voice. "This way, all you'll have to do is market your book and enjoy your family." She tipped her head. Let me help you. Let me . . . take over." She hoped her legs would hold up her quivering body. God help her if she hit the floor and passed out.

"And then who's going to run the kitchen?"

"Good question." Glenda shrugged when Mandie shot her a please-be-quiet glance.

"Shirley can handle it. She knows every inch of what I do. Has my schedule. And my shopping list. Knows when to order things. And I won't be far if she needs help."

Trey looked at his wife and nodded. "I think this could work."

Oh, bless you, Trey. C'mon, Syd, give me a chance.

"And then who would help Shirley? You know two people have to cook for weeklong retreats and family reunions."

Flustered, Mandie said, "I have a friend . . . who has a friend." Heat rose up her neck and seared the top of her head as she deflated like a collapsed cupcake. *What an idiotic answer.*

"A friend. Who has a friend? Really?" Sydney let out a slight grunt.

Shaking her head, Glenda muffled a chortle.

"Tell us about this friend. Of a friend." A smile inched up the corner of Trey's mouth. Sydney shot him a glare.

"Her name's Paula Warden. She's a trained chef and desperately needs a job. She's . . . um . . . Shirley's friend."

"So, Shirley knows you want the event planning job?" Sydney asked.

"Kind of, but not really." Mandie tried to corral her runaway thoughts. "Okay, yes. But only her. I've kept it to myself. For the most part." Did it really matter if she knew?

Trey hooked his thumbs in his pants pockets. "That's how you found Paula . . . ?"

"Warden. She's also a Colville tribal member. She's a go-getter."

"Have you met her?"

"No, but I trust Shirley."

Come on, come on. Say yes. Mandie shifted her weight, her pulse pounding in her ears.

"All right." Sydney's countenance softened. "We'll bring her in for an interview. And get me a list of your wedding ideas and plans. We're on a tight schedule. The wedding's going to be right before Christmas."

Okay. Let's see. Today's the sixth of December. Mandie spun her engagement ring around her finger. "How close to Christmas are we talking?"

"Christmas Eve." Sydney gave her a tight-lipped grin.

Christmas Eve. Okay. Mandie was sure her heart had just stopped.

"Can you handle planning both weddings?" Trey asked.

"Another good question." Glenda rocked in the padded office chair, her arms folded over her chest.

Mandie flipped her focus back on Sydney. "Piece of cake." Or she prayed it would be. Her attention swung to the ranch manifesto that hung on the wall alongside an aerial view of the three-generation-owned ranch and slid down to the fourth statement. *Make Goals and Prepare for the Ruts in the Road* stood out to her. Making goals was the simple part. She wasn't sure what ruts in the road would come her way, but with God as the official trail boss, everything would surely fall into place. As smooth as frosting. Right?

Sydney nodded, took another bite of cracker, and washed it down with a sip of Sprite. "Okay then. I'm going to give you your shot, Mandie Sellers. Only because I know you can handle it. And I know you're well organized. And yes, you are very, very creative. I'm going to give you a chance, just like people have given me."

"And pray," Trey said, "that Shirley and Paula can turn out food as tasty as yours."

"They will. You'll see." Mandie turned to Sydney and wagged a finger at her. "Thank you. You won't be disappointed."

"We're going to need lots of prayer to pull this off." Sydney glanced at the calendar on the wall. "You'll have eighteen days, minus Sundays."

Keeping her eyes on a document on the desk, Glenda quirked her brow and nodded. "Lots of prayer."

Mandie appreciated Sydney's flexibility and how she had a knack for going with the flow. And totally hand the reins over to God. Trusting God completely was something Mandie needed to work on. After thanking Sydney, Mandie practically skipped out of the office and found Hudson enjoying his steak dinner. She plopped down beside him and gave three gentle claps.

"You're not the only one with exciting news," Mandie said. "But I want to hear yours first."

Hudson wiped his mouth. "Okay, then." He set the napkin on the table. "I have a huge job offer at a lucrative environmental law firm in Seattle."

That was not the look Hudson Piccolo had expected to see on his beautiful fiancée's face. He thought she'd be excited. Thrilled even, thanking him, hugging him, showering him with kisses.

"This job will secure our future." She had to believe it. But her huckleberry eyes stated otherwise.

Mandie lowered her voice. "But you have a good job at the farm lending company."

He took in her cute ponytail with the festive red ribbon that held her sleek, dark brown hair in place. Took in her heart-shaped face. Her red Christmas sweater sported green trees. Her slight frame. "It might be a secure job, but it can be tough at times. Especially with the current economy. Telling folks they have to foreclose is not my idea of fun."

"I understand, but—"

"But what?" Hudson cringed at the too-high volume of his voice.

She fiddled with the cuff of her sweatshirt. "My big, exciting news is . . . I get my shot at being the event planner. Here." She leaned back and turned away with sadness in her eyes.

Hudson set his elbows on the table. "I know you've been wanting this job for a while now. And you should have it.

At least until I get this job and we move. After the wedding, that is." As soon as the words left his mouth, he regretted saying them.

Her face burned red, but she somehow held her composure. "You already have us moving? You want me to leave my family, settle away from my roots, away from my reservation? I've been here all my life."

"I understand your ties to your family and the land. But my roots are on the coast with *my* family. Well, my mom, anyhow." *God rest Dad's soul.* He pushed on. "With my culture that includes fishing. Your tribe's roots tie into salmon, right?"

She nodded.

"On the west side, you can fish all you want. We have hoards of salmon, and I get to help protect them for your family. For the people on your reservation. Doesn't that count for something?"

"You sound like you've already accepted the offer." Mandie played with her engagement ring, a silver-encased, two-carat, pear-shaped diamond. "Besides, we have hatcheries here that supply *my people* with plenty of salmon."

Touché. "No, I have not accepted the offer. But Gunner Randall from Puget Sound Council of Environmental Attorneys wants me to come and check out their firm. He's an all-star in the world of lawyers."

The knot in Mandie's belly squeezed. "When?"

"In the next week or two."

"What about planning our wedding? We have the cake tasting. We still have to pick out the music so Leena can rehearse."

"I'll help when I can. But that's girl stuff, isn't it?"

Mandie gave him a deep scowl. "Girl stuff? Really? Last time I checked, I'm not marrying anyone but you." Her countenance softened. "This is *our* wedding. We should be picking out these things together."

Hudson reached over and laced his fingers through hers. "Babe. This is a job of a lifetime. It will secure our future. And give Nona funds for the best education. A private school and the college of her choice. We're not going to get that here. We don't have the same opportunities in Omak or Nespelem that we could have in Seattle."

"But status and notoriety aren't everything. We've had lawyers and those getting their doctorates come off the rez. And money isn't everything, either. It doesn't buy happiness." Mandie glanced at her hands. "Besides, I just can't leave my family. I'm sorry." Nearly in tears, she pulled her hand out of his. "I'm going to get something to eat." She dashed for the kitchen.

Hudson sank back in his chair and let a sharp breath explode out of his mouth. Why everything had to be about her and her reservation and her people and her roots was beyond him. What about his culture? His family? He sacrificed a lot moving over here for her.

Trey sat down across from him, wearing a blue button-up and well-worn black cowboy boots. "How's it going out here?"

"Not as well as I'd imagined." Hudson took off his Stetson and set it on the table, then ran his fingers through his coarse hair.

"Did Mandie tell you about her planning this last-minute wedding?"

Hudson pushed his plate away. "Yeah. But that's not what's upsetting her. I'm happy she got the job. She'll be an amazing event planner. She's talented and good with people. Not to mention organized."

"Then what's the problem? If you don't mind me asking."

"I got a job offer."

"Congratulations, buddy. Where at?" Trey crossed his cowboy boot over his opposite ankle.

"Seattle."

Trey peaked a brow. "I don't imagine Mandie took the news very well."

Hudson grunted. "She made it clear moving's not an option."

Trey looked as though he was calculating his next remark. "She's been through a lot."

"I understand her upbringing and the ties to her family."

"It's more than her upbringing."

Maybe. But still. "This job can secure our future. She would never have to work if she didn't want to."

"And if she does?"

"Having a career is fine. It's her choice. I'm not going to make her be a stay-at-home mom." Hudson chuckled. "You know Mandie. Nobody tells her what to do."

"True. But her stubbornness and independence can be a positive quality because she doesn't let anybody run over the top of her. I think she stopped that a handful of years ago."

"Guess I have a lot to think about."

"I'll be praying for you both." Trey motioned to Hudson's plate. "Do you want a to-go box?"

"At least for the apple pie."

Trey reached over and clapped Hudson's shoulder. "You got it." He scooped up the plate and took it to the kitchen.

A long, snowy thirty minutes later, Hudson pulled up to his driveway, parked beside his one-story, bleak, undecorated house, and trudged inside the cold, simple living room. He tossed his to-go box on the coffee table and lit a fire in the woodstove. He still couldn't believe Mandie didn't hear him out. Or that she jumped up and left. He'd been excited. Thought she'd be too.

He shed his coat, cowboy boots, and Stetson, then plopped onto his couch and called his mom.

"Hey, Hudson, how are you, sweet boy? Are you guys getting snow out there? Looks like it, according to the radar."

Lauren Piccolo was a force to be reckoned with. One reason Hudson tried to make her happy. The other being that she was a recent widow. Last May, a heart attack ripped Dad out of their lives. Left Mom emotionally scattered in the wind, though she'd never admit it.

"I'm doing all right. Yeah, it's snowing pretty good here. I just got in."

Worry threaded through her voice. "You sound kind of down."

"My day started out well. Then got better with a job offer."

"But?"

"I told Mandie about it."

"And?"

"She's pretty adamant about not moving." Hudson planted his feet on the pine coffee table.

Mom's voice piqued interest and hope. "Moving? Where to? Who offered you the job?"

"Gunner Randall called this afternoon. He wants to interview me for a job in his law firm."

"I know Gunner. He's from Puget Sound Council. His firm is loaded with skilled attorneys working on important cases. Did he offer you the job? Or does he want an interview?"

"It sounded like he offered me the job. But I'm sure it's an interview. He wants me to come over in a week or two to check out the offices and tell me about some of the cases they're working on."

"What are the cases involved with?"

"Salmon protection in surrounding lakes and streams."

"How exciting. He's a good man. A powerful man. You're going to have to find a way to convince Mandie to move over here. This is too good of an opportunity to pass up. You have your future to think of. I'd hate to have a woman hold you back."

Was she kidding? "But not just any woman. Right, Mom? You're talking about her being Native American."

Mom's voice turned sharp. "What are you talking about?"

"You've never liked her because she's not a rich, white woman."

"That is not true, Hudson, and you know it."

"Then what's the issue?"

"To be honest, she's no Blair Buchanan."

Blair? Hudson clenched his jaw. "You mean the woman who left me for someone more impressive? Someone further along in his career? That Blair?"

"He's not put a ring on her finger." Mom's tone went syrupy. "Besides, she's perfect for you, honey. She's a fellow attorney with grace and style, and she's a woman who's going places with big goals and dreams. She's from a prestigious family. Race has nothing to do with it. With Blair, you'd be in the same class, and there would be no conflicts."

Her socialite attitude and the mention of his ex reminded him of why he left Seattle. "You're going to have to get over the class issue, Mom. I love Mandie, not Blair. The only thing I'm concerned about right now is to figure out what's best for my family."

Mom's tone softened. "I want you to be with the woman you love. And I like Mandie. I do. She's adorable. But—"

"Good. Because she's the woman I plan to marry."

"Oh, Hudson. I just want you to be happy. I've only ever wanted you to be happy."

"I am happy, Mom. Especially with Mandie and Nona."

"But you're not happy in your job, are you?"

"It's not my dream job, that's for sure." Watching people lose their livelihoods in foreclosure was the pits. He stared through the glass door of the now blazing woodstove.

"Then come over. Check out the job. There's no harm in that, is there? We can go to dinner. I need to see you. I miss you, son."

"I miss you too. I'll come and check out the job. At least see what my future could hold."

Glee shone through Mom's tone. "That's my boy. You tell me when and I'll pick you up at the airport. You can stay with me in the condo."

In the condo. Without Dad. "I can't believe he's been gone for seven months." The first heart attack was bad enough. But when the second one came and stole his life, his death took a toll on him and Mom. If only he had siblings to share the grief with.

"Is that why you don't come over as often? Because your father's not here?"

"I've been busy at work. And with Mandie and Nona." Though he did have a hard time being there without Dad's encouragement. He always had a good time talking about his caseload with the man he admired most.

Thank goodness he had Mandie and her big, loving family. They accepted him as he was—a city man trying to make it in the country. Wearing a cowboy hat and boots.

"Let me know when you're coming."

"Will do."

After hanging up with Mom, he called Mandie, not wanting to leave the night in disarray.

"Hey, babe."

"Hey, sweetness. Sorry I got up and left like I did. It was wrong and rude. But I can't move. Can't see myself living anywhere else. I'm a country girl at heart. I hate the city. It makes me feel claustrophobic and stresses me out. I love it here. I love working on the ranch. Living in my small house with Nona. I love you, but . . ."

Mandie's voice brightened. "I needed to hear you say that. I love you so much. I can't lose you. And if you're not happy in your job, then no, I don't want you to stay there. But I don't want to move either." She let out a deep sigh. "This is hard."

"Yes, it is. But we'll figure it out. I'll call Mr. Randall in the morning and let him know I'm coming to simply check out my options. Can we agree on that?"

Mandie hesitated. Then in her brave-as-usual voice, she said, "Yeah, we can. In the meantime, maybe you can see what your options are around here too. Like, possibly going out on your own. You could have a home office right here in Nespelem."

The idea of going out on his own made him recoil. "There's a lot at stake when starting your own business. It would be as hectic as working in a big law firm. And I wouldn't have the financial security of working for someone else."

Financial security was his number one priority. Knowing Mandie had grown up poor, he had to make sure she'd never be there again.

CHAPTER 2

Mandie felt Hudson slipping away like all the other men in her life had. Starting with her favorite uncle, Sam, who died in a car accident when she was nine. Then her high school sweetheart for another prettier, athletic girl. Her daughter's worthless father had bolted when he heard about the pregnancy, conceived before Mandie had come to Christ. And now Hudson, who wanted to move across the state.

She doubted he'd ever leave her and Nona behind, but still, the triggers were real. She hated how they could leave her feeling hopeless. Hated how they kept her awake at night. Hated the ache they caused in her belly.

Her five-year-old daughter padded into Mandie's bedroom with a look of concern on her face. Their home was a small HUD house near the Colville Tribal Headquarters in Nespelem. But it was her house, and it was warm and cozy.

"Mommy, why do you look so sad?" Wearing pink pajamas with candy canes on them, Nona crawled into bed beside Mandie.

Mandie knuckled tears away from her eyes. "I'm fine, sweetheart. I'm just happy because I get to plan a wedding at Auntie Sydney's ranch."

Nona's face brightened. "That's fun, Mommy. Can I help?"

"Of course you can. You can help me once school's out. You have two more weeks, and then you're on Christmas vacation. Won't that be fun?"

"I can help you make the pouquets. I love flowers."

Mandie let out a soft chuckle. "Yes, you can help me make the *bouquets*. You can help me tie the ribbons around the flowers."

"Yay!" Nona flipped the covers off and jumped on the bed. Then she settled down and snuggled with her mom.

Mandie wrapped her arms around her little girl, holding on to the one person she believed would never abandon her.

Nona reached over and fetched a children's Bible off a nightstand. "Will you read me a story?"

"I would love to." Mandie read the story of Esther, emphasizing how the queen was made for such a time as this. She had to believe that she was made for planning weddings. When finished, she found Nona fast asleep in her arms.

Mandie kissed the little girl's head and slipped out of bed, careful not to wake her. She went to the kitchen table where her three-inch event planning book rested and thumbed through the pages. She stopped on a page that reflected what Holly Sinclair's Winter Wonderland theme might look like. Soft blue lights, silver candleholders, blue-and-white flowers and star ornaments. A bride in her lace wedding gown with a furry ivory stole around her shoulders. The rest of the wedding party wearing smoky blue attire.

It all made her even more eager to marry the man of her dreams.

After finding paper and a pencil, she started to list what the bride would need. Flowers. Music. Menu. Cake. Number of guests. Favorite colors. All Sydney had shared was the Winter Wonderland theme in white, silver, and blue. Hopefully, Mandie would get the bride's file tomorrow.

An hour later, she yawned and slid in beside Nona. Her mind vacillated between the letdown of Hudson's desire to move and the excitement of planning a Christmas wedding.

Vow Day was in eighteen working days, minus Sundays. God help her.

After dropping Nona off at kindergarten the next day, Mandie drove through the white-tipped sagebrush to the ivory blanket covering Seven Tine Guest Ranch's pasture-land a couple of miles north of the town of Nespelem, which was five minutes north of the Colville Tribe's Agency. The sky shone blue and held a crispness in the air. She parked, grabbed her Southwestern notebook-filled bag, and trekked into the two-story, fifteen-room log guest lodge.

Inside the warm foyer, maple syrup and sausage teased her taste buds. She shed her layers, slipped her feet into a pair of black clogs, and dropped her bag in the ranch office. Now for the wedding file. She had seventeen days to plan. Not finding the folder, she crept to the kitchen so she wouldn't disturb the attorneys and their retreat on the couch and chairs by the crackling fireplace.

"Hey, Shirls." She donned her Christmas gift–embellished apron and looked at the lunch menu. "How'd breakfast go?"

"It went well. It helped to have everything prepped the night before. And I had help this morning." Shirley wiped her hands on her cupcake-embroidered apron and moved away from the sink.

"You had help. Who?"

"Paula Warden. Who else?"

"She's here?" A line of lit, decorated miniature Christmas trees along the counter between the two sets of batwing doors caught Mandie's attention. *Nice addition.*

"Yes. Sydney had me call her last night."

"Well, where is she?"

Shirley leaned against the lengthy wooden island. "She went to Omak for additional supplies."

"Why? We're well-stocked. What's she picking up?"

"We just found out that one of the female attorneys is a vegetarian."

"Got it." Mandie went to the fridge and found a clear plastic bag of Sydney's famous teriyaki dried deer meat. She plopped a morsel into her mouth.

"Paula really wants this job. She loves the ranch. Loves Sydney and Trey. Met them before Sydney and her aunt headed to Spokane."

A twinge of unexpected territorial jealousy thumped Mandie's chest. But she smiled anyway. "That's wonderful." *Bless us all. This might just work out as planned.*

"I'll start prepping lunch then." Shirley went back to the sink and washed a muffin tin.

"What's on the menu?"

"Beef sandwiches and au jus. Garden salad. And Shanghai bok choy for the vegetarian." Shirley scrubbed another muffin tin.

"Sounds yummy."

"I found the recipe on Pinterest after she mentioned she has an affinity for oriental meals."

Mandie perused the rest of the week's menu, which included meals for Thursday through Sunday. She checked off Wednesday's breakfast. "I see today's lunch dessert includes snickerdoodle cookies. I'll make those if you want to tackle tonight's pumpkin pies."

"We've got things covered in here." Shirley dried her hands on a dish towel and tossed it on the counter. "You have a wedding to plan. Congrats, by the way."

"Thanks." Mandie regarded the time on her cell phone. Nine o'clock in the morning. "Sydney won't be back until six or so with these slick roads." She hated waiting. "She didn't leave me any instructions to get started." Her cell rang, and Sydney's number flashed on the screen. *Oh good.* Mandie answered the call. "Hey. How are the roads?"

"They're not too bad. How's Paula doing so far?"

"Shirley said she did a knockout job at breakfast. She went to Omak to pick up supplies. Did you know we have a vegetarian in the group?"

"I did not. Sounds like you guys have everything under control."

"As always." She wanted to ask Sydney about the wedding plans but didn't want to push her.

"Hey, I wanted to let you know I left you a folder on my desk with Holly Sinclair's cell number. Please get ahold of her this morning and start planning. Everything you need is in the file."

Of course it is. She should never have doubted Sydney. "Great. I'll get started right away."

"All righty then. I'm getting carsick, so I'm going to hang up. Let me know if you need anything."

"Will do. Be safe." Mandie ended the call.

Shirley leaned against the counter with a smile on her face. She folded her arms across her chest. "This is your dream job, isn't it?"

"Ever since I was a little girl. Never thought it'd come true though."

"Paula and I have the kitchen covered. Go live your dream."

Mandie hugged Shirley. And with a bounce in her step, she wove through the dining tables and into the office. She sank into Sydney's desk chair, feeling empowered—even valued because Sydney was trusting her at a whole new level. She giggled and found the file under the current issue of *Cowgirls and Wildflowers*. She opened the folder.

"First name, last name, phone number. Good. Where she lives. Favorite colors are blue, purple, and red. But since this is a Winter Wonderland theme, she's going with blue, silver, and white hues. The best man and groomsmen will be in dark blue tuxes and white shirts." She tapped the folder. *This is going to be a beautiful wedding.*

After Mandie made the call and confirmed the notes with Holly, she picked up a call from Hudson.

"Hey, babe. What day are we tasting cake and choosing songs?"

Mandie giggled. "We are choosing songs tomorrow with Leena. And we're tasting cake . . . hang on." She checked the calendar on her cell phone. "Next Wednesday at one."

"I still wish you'd bake our cake. You're the best cake-maker in the world."

"That's sweet, honey. But no bride wants to make her own wedding cake."

"I get it." Hudson chuckled. "I'm going to call Mr. Randall and book my flight."

Book my flight. Mandie's muscles tightened. It sounded far away. She made herself sound upbeat. "Thanks for letting me know."

"Love you."

"Love you more."

She smiled when Hudson said, "Love you most."

She ended the call. She'd have to dig deep and trust that he would not move to Seattle and abandon her. Stupid triggers. They'd had many conversations about his job, but she didn't realize he'd been so miserable. Poor guy. She'd have to do something extra special for him. Like cook him a nice dinner or bake his favorite cake.

Trey entered the office with his two-year-old son, Lester, dangling face down over his shoulder. His little legs kicked the air. "I brought you an assistant." Lester giggled and wiggled as Trey tickled his side. He righted the boy in his arms and held him as though he were a human football. The toddler's squinty eyes exuded sheer joy.

"How much are you going to charge me an hour?" Mandie asked Lester.

"No." Lester scrunched his face.

"Perfect. I'll take free help anytime."

"No." Lester shook a chubby finger at her.

"Use your manners." Trey tipped him upside down. "Say 'No thank you.'"

"No thank you." The boy wagged his head, shaking his entire body.

Trey set his son on his shoulders. "Will you watch this monkey for me? His babysitter should be here in about five."

"I sure can." Mandie rose from the desk, grateful for a distraction from Hudson's plans to fly to Seattle. She wanted to be mad at him, but an image of how hot he looked last night in his Western button-up shirt and brown cowboy boots before she ditched him at the dining room table settled in her mind. She took the wiggle worm from Trey and plopped him on her hip. "Let's go get a snack." She turned her attention to Trey. "Have a good photo shoot. It's a great day for one."

"It sure is. I'll see you in a couple hours."

Mandie followed him out of the office and veered toward the kitchen. "Let's see what we can rustle up to eat. Are you hungry for cheese and crackers or peanut butter and celery?"

Lester waved his left hand in the air as they strode through the batwing doors. "Yeah."

Mandie kissed his soft cheek and settled Lester at a children's table in the kitchen with crackers and cheese and a sippy cup of milk.

Shirley stood at the island rolling out pie dough and listening to "Silver Bells" playing on her cell phone. "What are you doing with this sweet child?" She gave the boy a bright smile.

"Waiting for the babysitter. She should be here any minute."

"I can watch him until she arrives. That way you can get started."

"Are you sure?"

"Absolutely." Shirley winked at Lester. "You'll stay in here with me, right, buddy?"

Not paying attention to the women, Lester bobbed his head to the music as he enjoyed his snack.

"Perfect. I'll see you later." Mandie pushed through the doors as Sunny, her younger sister, walked toward her from the foyer. "He's in the kitchen having a snack with Shirley."

"Is he in a good mood today?" Sunny peered at the group of attorneys who were mingling by the fire and in the gift shop, obviously taking a break.

"So far I've gotten two noes and a yeah."

"Oh, a step up from last week's screaming fit in Safeway. Lucky you."

As they walked past each other, the ladies high-fived, and Mandie strode to the office. She gathered a corkboard, a box of dry-erase pens, a roll of paper towels, and an easel from the office closet, then nabbed the folder and her bag. Humming a Christmas tune, she set her supplies by the door in the foyer while she bundled into her coat, hat, gloves, and tan winter boots. Then she headed to the loft above the hay barn.

An hour later and with a fire blazing in the woodstove, she had her workspace set up, which included a storyboard filled with wedding ideas and her colorful sketches from earlier this morning. She strode around the room. If only there was something special to add to the loft.

Minutes later, she called Trey. "How many Christmas trees can the loft hold?"

Trey laughed.

Mandie set her free hand on her hip. "Humor me."

"Maybe five or six."

"I'm sorry. Did you say ten or fifteen?"

"Ten or fifteen? Good grief, Mandie. What are you planning?"

Mandie slowly twirled. "A very special something for the bride-to-be."

Trey grunted. "You or the other gal?"

"The other gal." *Duh.*

"Fine. Go with ten."

Mandie scoffed. "Fifteen it is . . . if some of them are pencil trees."

"What the heck is a pencil tree?"

Mandie looked up a photo from the internet and texted it to him. "I just sent you an image."

"Got it." A pause. "Yes. Fifteen trees will fit *if* most of them are pencil trees."

"Perfect. We can cut most of the Christmas trees the week before and decorate them so they release their fresh pine scent right before the nuptials. In the meantime, I'll order a handful of pencil trees. Shall I use your credit card?" When a laugh escaped her, she pressed a fist to her mouth.

"You can use yours and I'll reimburse you. Maybe."

"The ranch credit card it is." Her screen went dark. For kicks, she sent Trey one smiley face and fifteen Christmas tree emojis. Tickled with herself, she took out her sketch pad and colored pencils and added fifteen trees to the outline of the loft.

Footsteps pounded up the wooden staircase, and Shirley appeared with a thermos, an insulated mug, and a cloth shopping bag. "How are things going in here?"

Mandie pointed to her storyboard. "I think I'm off to a good start."

Shirley crossed the room and stopped in front of Mandie's setup. "I'd say you are. Tell me about these sketches. Do you think Trey will approve of this many trees?"

"Just talked to him. They're basically ordered." At least in her mind they were. All she had to do was get the okay from Sydney with a quick text. Which she did and received a thumbs up. *Yay. I'm good to go.*

Shirley chuckled. "Good for you. Pies are in the oven. What do you want for lunch?"

"Honestly, soup and salad sound good to me."

"Me too. I'll go make us some beef and vegetable soup."

"Perfect. I'll walk you back to the lodge and order the trees."

"I thought you already ordered them."

Mandie donned her jacket. "All I have to do is add the credit card number and push the Order button."

Inside the lodge, Shirley headed toward the kitchen and Mandie to the office. After settling into the comfy office chair, Mandie fired up the laptop, entered the four-digit passcode, and found the webpage for the Christmas trees. She might not look like an event planner at the moment, but she sure felt like one.

She leaned closer to the screen and went to put in the desired quantity. The number available caught her attention. *Only two left. Great. Now what?*

By early afternoon, Hudson sat at a small desk in a worn office chair, drafting loan agreements and promissory notes for a few Okanogan Farm Lending Firm farming clients.

He imagined being on one of the top floors of a downtown Seattle skyscraper in a plush Puget Sound Council of Environmental Attorneys' office.

Yeah, he could almost smell the lobster dinners at a fine restaurant. See a classy waitress serving up sweet, rich desserts. Feel Mandie sitting next to him, dressed in form-fitting gowns and high heels, her nails painted and manicured and as beautifully done as Mom's.

He had hardly slept last night and was already on his second pot of hot, black coffee. Torn between staying in small-town America and leaving for a city rich in history and culture, his dreams volleyed between being with Mandie and the hurt Blair Buchanan had caused him. Blair. What a mess. He could never be with such a snooty, self-involved woman like her. Why couldn't Mom see that? Blair could never replace Mandie's kind, caring ways. Besides, his ex had never looked at him like Mandie did.

He picked up his phone and entered Gunner Randall's cell number from his email. His pulse pounded in his ears. He got up and paced until the man's voice boomed through the speaker.

"Hudson. Great to hear from you, buddy. How are things in Omak?"

He smiled at the warm greeting and settled back in his chair. "At the moment, pretty cold and white."

"I don't know how you deal with all the snow, let alone having to drive in it. That's what I love about the West side. We hardly get any of the slick white stuff. It's a bright blue day on this side of the Cascades."

Hudson did miss the mild winters. "Good to hear, sir."

"So, when can you come this way?"

Hudson leaned back. "Looks like I can come at the end of next week."

"Perfect. I look forward to meeting you."

"I look forward to meeting you, too, sir. And to see what you have to offer."

"We have big plans for you. I can't wait to tell you all about it. What I'm going to do, son, is transfer you over to my right-hand gal, and she's going to book your flight. I'll see you next week."

A mature but sweet-sounding female came on the line and noted the day Hudson said he would not be available to come. "I'll email you your confirmation here in a second . . . and we'll see you next Thursday."

Hudson thanked her and ended the call. *See you next Thursday.* If only it were tomorrow. Thirty minutes and another cup of joe later, he pulled up the confirmation email. *Oh no.* How could they have gotten it wrong? He called Mr. Randall back, but it went to voicemail.

Hudson did an internet search for Puget Sound Council and found a number for the main office. The same woman answered.

"Hey, this is Hudson Piccolo. I think there's been a mistake. I said I could *not* come on Wednesday."

"Yes. You did say that, but unfortunately, Mr. Randall had something come up and will be unavailable on Thursday, so we had to switch you to Wednesday. We'll see you next week, right?"

"I'd prefer to push it back to Friday." Mandie would kill him if he missed the cake-tasting day.

"Let me check Mr. Randall's schedule." Elevator music played in the background until she came back on. "It looks like Mr. Randall's booked on Friday. And for the next two weeks. After that, the time runs into the holidays. He says Wednesday is your only option."

How ridiculous. How could Wednesday be the only time they could meet? He rubbed his rattled head.

"There are other attorneys he's considering if that helps you decide."

Other attorneys? Mr. Randall led him to believe he was the only candidate and practically had the job in his back pocket. Why had he been deceptive?

"Mr. Piccolo, shall I keep Wednesday's flight scheduled for you?"

Maybe they could change the day of the cake testing. "Yes, keep the flight. I'll see you next Wednesday." When his screen went black, he swiped it and pulled up Mandie's cell number from his contact list. His finger hovered over the green Call button.

No, he had to talk to her face-to-face. He could duck out early. Stop at a client's farm on the way out of town. After letting his boss know he was leaving, Hudson jumped in his blue Chevy Colorado, dropped off some lending documents, and made a beeline to Seven Tine. But before going to the loft, he grabbed two to-go cups of hot cocoa from the ranch's coffee bar.

A burst of hot air and Mandie singing "Let it snow, let it snow, let it snow" along with her music app greeted him as he took the last step into the hayloft. Boxes of decorations littered the floor as did a corkboard with what looked like Mandie's sketches perched on an easel, and a single round table, no chairs, centered the room. She was so into what she was doing, his heavy footfalls clicking the floor past her pile of winter clothes hadn't even nabbed her attention.

"Hey, beautiful." He smiled, ready for a hug and a kiss, as he crossed the room.

Mandie gasped, screamed, and spun to face him, her eyes round. "What are you doing here?" She regarded the time on her cell phone. "At four in the afternoon?" She wiped stray hair out of her eyes. "Not that I'm sad to see you."

He set the to-go cups on the table and reached out a hand to help her up. "I came to see my gorgeous event planner."

Blushing, she grasped his hand, stood, and gave him a hug. "I'm glad you came."

"You've been busy." She looked adorable with her dark-brown hair up in a clip and the loose ends framing her face. He liked her red-and-white sweater with "Merry" on the front. He also liked her green-and-red holiday socks that stuck out of her jeans. Her half-eaten lunch sat next to a roll of paper towels.

"You have no idea." She stepped back and spoke with her hands thrashing the air. "I tried to order pencil trees to go with the array of cut ones after Trey okayed me finagling fifteen various-sized trees in here." She swept her arms around the room. "But when I went to order them off the website, there were only two left. Can you believe only two?"

"No. I can't." He chuckled at how animated she was.

"It's the beginning of December, for crying out loud. There should be way more than that. But, I was able to order two more off a different website, but that's still not enough. I need more. I'll have to make a run out to Hobby Lobby in Spokane and see if they have any. And maybe Michael's too. Can you drive me out there Saturday? We could make a family trip of it. Take Nona. Have lunch. Twigs sounds good. Oh, or P. F. Chang's. What do you think?"

"Saturday, huh? Hey, maybe we could taste the cake and kill two birds with one stone." *Oh, yeah. Brilliant idea.*

Mandie tipped her chin upward. Squinted at him. "Taste the cake on a Saturday. When you know we're scheduled to do it Wednesday. What's up with that?"

Hudson took her hands in his and kissed the top of her left hand. "There was a tiny glitch with Mr. Randall's schedule. The only day he can meet with me is Wednesday."

"Oh." Mandie's countenance collapsed. "But you know that's the day we're tasting the cake options. You promised you would be there. You said you didn't want anyone else to plan our wedding but us." She shrugged her shoulders. "Your words, not mine." Her tone was soft, honest, filled with disappointment.

Which jabbed at his chest. He rubbed her hand with his thumb. "This isn't what I planned, but it's the only day Mr. Randall can get with me. I tried, babe. I told his secretary that I would not be available on Wednesday. But it's the only day he had available, and come to find out, they're looking at more candidates, not just me. This might be my only shot."

Mandie nodded. "I do understand what it feels like to get a single chance."

He hated the moisture pooling in her eyes. She blinked several times, appearing to fight off her emotions. He wrapped his arms around her and took in her dark, beautiful eyes. "Thank you for understanding. I'm simply going to take a look at my options. And find out if I can work some—or much—of the time from home."

"Hopefully most of the time." Shifting her weight, she accidentally bumped the table with her hip and knocked over the to-go cup. The cup, lid, and contents splattered the floor. In seconds, brown liquid raced for the papers she had spread out. The cocoa reached the documents and lapped them up. "No, no, no." She broke Hudson's hold on her and dropped to her knees, then picked up the papers and tried to dry them on her jeans.

"Are they ruined?"

Mandie shook her head. "I don't think so."

Hudson helped her mop up the mess with paper towels from the box of supplies on the floor. "Remember, this is a huge law firm. I might not get to choose how much I could work from home."

"If at all." She spread her papers out on a dry section of the floor.

"Please call and see if we can taste the cake either on our way to or from Spokane on Saturday or any other day but Wednesday." He crouched in front of her and rested his hands on her slight shoulders. "I want to plan our wedding together, and I want to taste cake with you. But this is my only chance. Please."

Though still appearing bummed, she nodded. "You're right. I get my shot at event planning. You should have your turn to go for a job you really want. I'll make the call and see if we can change the day."

Hudson tamped down his excitement, not wanting to rub anything in her nose. But he did kiss it. And then kissed her cheek and her fingers. "Love you."

She said it, but not with her normal enthusiasm. "Love you more."

"Love you most." Hopefully, she believed him.

CHAPTER 3

The realization of having a mere seventeen days to plan one wedding and tie up loose ends with hers—without the much-needed help of her fiancé or anyone else—weighed heavy on Mandie's shoulders. Her notes were a sopping mess. Awesome.

She chewed on her bottom lip. Maybe they should reschedule their wedding for February. Or spring. Or summer. June is nice. She sank to the floor, wishing she had a chair, wincing at the thought of moving her wedding.

Christmas music playing from her cell phone didn't help relieve her frustration over her drenched notes. Hudson eased down beside her with a piece of the chocolate cake Mandie had made him that morning. "How can I help you?" He took a bite.

"Besides staying here and not flying to Seattle?" She cringed and chided her less-than-festive tone. "Sorry." Hudson didn't deserve a sour reply. He'd bent over backward with his busy schedule to help her with the wedding. She needed to support him like he supported her.

Hudson let out an exasperated sigh and set his empty paper plate on the floor.

"I'm glad you're here."

He gave her a small smile. "Me too."

She dropped to her elbows, mad at herself for hurting his feelings. "To answer your question, I need to set up four easels. Two of them will hold wedding storyboards and two will hold whiteboards for the schedules. That way I can check off what's been done and know what hasn't."

"Where are the other two easels? I'll get them for you."

"I think they're in the storage room behind the gift shop."

Hudson gathered the soiled paper towels and the paper plate and stood. "I'll go see what I can find. Do you need markers too?"

"Yes, please."

He studied her for a moment. "Everything's going to be okay. We just need to pray and trust God and His will."

Easier said than done. But he was right. "Yes, we do." Through the sensation of a weighted blanket across her shoulders, she forced a happy face.

After Hudson left, Mandie rolled to her knees and picked up the notes to reorganize them. With another paper towel, she tried to wick the remaining moisture out of the paper. When satisfied, she plopped her supply box on the table and retrieved sticky notes and colored markers.

Twenty minutes later, Hudson returned with two whiteboards, two easels, and a box full of additional dry-erase markers, paper towels, and two fresh to-go insulated cups of cocoa. He handed a cup to her and set the supplies on the floor. "Yours has an extra splash of pumpkin spice creamer."

Her heart melted. His thoughtfulness is what she loved most about him. He definitely had a servant's heart. "You're a gem." She took a sip.

Shirley entered the loft, a plastic storage container in hand, and glanced around at the decorations, notes, and lights strung out on the wooden floor. "How's it going in here?"

"Truth be told, I'm off to a rough start." Mandie held her mug in the air as though offering a salute. "Which means the day can only get better."

Shirley set the container on a table, gave Mandie a hug, and whispered, "I'm praying for you." She nodded to Hudson and left.

Hudson returned Shirley's nod and turned to Mandie. "I could use one of those."

She creased her eyebrows. "Use one of what?"

He opened his arms. "A hug."

She took another sip of her cocoa, letting the warm pumpkin flavor settle on her tongue. Then she swallowed and stepped into Hudson's secure embrace.

"Me too." She rested her head on his chest.

He rubbed her back and kissed the side of her head. Inhaled the scent of her shampoo. "I believe in you and know you can make the bride's wedding a very special event."

"Which bride are you talking about?" She lifted her chin and gave him a playful grin.

"Both of them." Hudson released her and stepped backward. "Where do you want these?" He pointed to the supplies he'd fetched for her.

Mandie set her hand on her hip. "Leave them there. I'll take care of it."

"I'll let you get back to work. Let me know if you need anything else. I can always make a run to the variety store in Coulee Dam for you."

"Where are you off to?"

"I have time to check on a new client down the road."

Mandie nodded. "Okay. Go get 'em, tiger." She took a sip. "I'll let you know if I run out of something." And that's why she didn't want to wait till February. His thoughtfulness and willingness attracted her to him like a magnet, even if the job he planned on pursuing happened to be on the other side of the state. He was a good, good man.

Help us figure things out, Lord.

She watched him don his jacket and disappear down the stairs. *Help me trust that amazing man.* She had to trust that God had the perfect plan for her and Nona. *"His will, way, and timing."* Something Sydney had drilled into her through the years. Darn if His timing didn't slap Mandie in the derriere every time.

For King + Country came on singing "Little Drummer Boy." The remarkable version they'd played live at CMT Country Christmas. She turned up the volume, took another sip of cocoa, stoked the fire, and went to work.

She listed seventeen days and tasks for each one, then included what both brides, Holly and she, already had in place and what still needed to be done. After nearly an hour of work, she stepped back and folded her arms across her chest. To fill in the blanks on the whiteboard schedule, she had to talk to Holly.

She snatched her cell phone off the floor and tapped in the bride's number from the file. A voicemail message came on and Mandie said, "Hey, this is Mandie Sellers from Seven Tine Guest Ranch. I need more information on what flowers you want in case I can't get them. Also, can I get your guest list and menu? And please let me know what day and time everyone is arriving so I can nail down the timeline for Vow Day. One more thing, could you get me the groom's cell phone number? Please call me back so we can set up a time to meet. I look forward to working with you."

She had an hour before picking Nona up from school. To fill the time, she added to her schedule. Not long after she started, boot steps clunked up the stairway and a haggard Shirley appeared.

She took a moment to catch her breath. "The stove quit working, and I don't know what to do. I've got a special bean soup simmering for the vegetarian tonight. It's going to take several more hours to cook on low heat, which is best, and

I need more time. And now, if I put it in the slow cooker, it won't get done."

"Let me see if Tucker's available to check it out."

"Perfect. I saw him go into the barn on my way here."

Mandie bent over and set her markers on the floor, donned her winter attire, and followed Shirley outside. "Why don't you go find out what else she might like for dinner, and I'll go find Tucker."

"I'll let you know what she decides."

"Sounds good." Mandie trotted to the barn and opened the door. Inside the eight-stall structure, horses poked their noses out of their stalls. Some greeted her with whinnies. She found Tucker in the heated tack room, oiling saddles and listening to country music.

"Hey. The stove quit working. Shirley has a soup on that needs to slow cook. Do you have time to go check it out?"

"Sure." The ranch hand wiped his hands on a rag and set it on the counter. "I don't know why they keep that old thing. Isn't it the original stove Sydney's grandpa installed?"

"I think so." Mandie snickered. "She does have a hard time giving up family heirlooms." Which Mandie completely understood after the sudden death of her boss's parents five years ago. She followed the ranch hand to Seven Tine's kitchen. Barbecue scented the room. At the island counter, Paula made homemade rolls as a country song drifted from a cell phone.

"Smells good in here." Mandie stopped at the island, and Tucker went to the stove. "How are things working out for you, Paula?"

"Other than the stove burners breaking down, all is well." Paula glanced at a recipe card. "I hope the oven will stay on. I don't know what we'll do if the ribs don't get cooked."

"Plan B for me usually includes the two grills out back." Mandie nodded to the door leading outside and to the main house that belonged to Trey and Sydney.

"Thanks for the tip." Paula added sugar and salt to the bowl of the KitchenAid mixer.

"One of them's a Traeger."

"Even better." Paula added warm milk.

Shirley swung through the doors and breezed into the kitchen. "Our guest was looking forward to the bean soup. But said a vegetable would go along with a grilled cheese sandwich."

"No way am I serving her grilled cheese when everybody else is having a rib dinner." Paula scratched her cheek with her shoulder. "I have a vegetarian friend who makes these delicious avocado and tomato sandwiches. I'll fix her one of those."

Tucker stood after examining the stovetop. "Honestly, I don't know what's wrong with this dinosaur. I think it's a hunk of junk that needs to go to the dump."

"What am I going to do?" Shirley slapped her hand on the counter.

"You'll have to take it to the main house," Mandie said.

"Why didn't we think of that earlier?" Shirley said to Paula.

"Good question." The wall clock suggested Mandie leave now to pick up Nona from the after-school program. "The front door should be unlocked. You can work in there, Shirls." She turned to Paula. "God willing the oven will stay on. Trey and Sydney should be back with Leena in a few hours."

"You two good?" Mandie's attention swiveled between the two cooks.

"We're dandy." Shirley lifted the pot off the stove and headed for the door. The ranch hand rushed over, opened it, and followed her outside.

Paula watched them leave, then turned back to Mandie. "I didn't think about using the main house's kitchen."

"Don't worry about it. You'll learn how to be flexible in no time." When Tucker came back inside, Mandie said, "I'll let Trey know and see what he wants to do. I need to go get Nona. Thanks for your help, you guys."

They said in unison, "You're welcome." Then glanced at each other affectionately.

"Watch out. This ranch has a way of matchmaking," Mandie mumbled as she pushed through the doors and headed for her white Toyota Highlander.

When inside, she called Trey. But there was no answer, so she left a message to call either her or his ranch hand. It would be a miracle if there was a simple trick to get the stove up and running again.

She started the engine and turned up the heat before praying that nothing else would derail her day.

Hudson sat across from Mandie at her kitchen table, trying to figure out how to get her to be more excited about the possible new job with the Puget Sound Council of Environmental Attorneys and maybe a move across the state.

He took a bite of his favorite huckleberry pie with whipped cream she'd made him for dessert.

They had just enjoyed a nice spaghetti dinner. And now, Nona played with her stuffed animals on the floor in the living room while a *Blue's Clues* episode played in the background.

He stared at the Christmassy floral piece with tiny lights flickering and dancing inside a glass vase centered on the table and listened to Mandie recount the day's events.

"I'm glad the bean soup survived. I have an old propane camp stove you guys can set up outside. Let me know if you need it." His mind wandered back to the job offer. In all honesty, they were having such a lovely time, he didn't even want to bring it up and ruin the night.

"I will. Thanks." Mandie rubbed the back of her neck. "This is all too much. I don't know what I was thinking, taking on two weddings in less than a month. I know ours is mostly finished, but still, it's a lot."

"This's what you want, though. Right? To be an event planner."

She gave him a look. "True."

"Nobody said it would be easy, right?"

"Correct."

"You're a super organizer. A hard worker. Dedicated. Smart. Beautiful."

She tossed him a sassy smile. "All of it's true." She shrugged and turned serious. "But I feel like I'm on a runaway horse, bareback, with no bridle."

He nodded. "What are your options?"

She grunted. "I guess I have to suck it up and keep going. I'm not going to give up planning Holly's wedding."

"Why don't you ask your family for help?"

"Because it's my job, not theirs."

"Our wedding isn't your job."

"No, but my mom and Marlee are busy with work." She wished her older sister was available. Her mom too. She'd love to spend more time with them.

"What about Sunny? She doesn't work full-time."

"She's busy helping me with Nona in her free time." Mandie burst out laughing. "Plus, she can't wrap a present for the life of her. She uses gift bags." She massaged her temples. "Besides, they plan to take the week off between

Christmas and New Year's Eve. I'm hoping their 'help' won't be more of a hindrance."

Hudson was about to walk on fire. But the idea that just popped into his head was better than watching Mandie fret. "What about changing ours?"

"I'll admit the thought has crossed my mind." She furrowed her brows. "But I don't want to wait any longer than I have to, to marry you."

"I don't want to wait either. But as stressed out as you're getting, and only two days in—"

Her tone bit. "I'm not one to quit."

"But the two weddings are weighing on you. Is it worth it?" He dug deeper, recoiling with each necessary statement. "Remember, when you're stressed, Nona's stressed. When you're stressed, I'm stressed. When you're stressed—"

"Okay, okay." Mandie held up a hand and laughed. "I get it. But I'm not going to postpone our wedding."

"We can always get married on Valentine's. Isn't that the most romantic day of the year?" Or so he'd heard.

Mandie picked up her spoon and chucked it at him.

The utensil nailed him in the chest and clinked to the floor. "Really, Mandie?"

"I can handle it. I'm merely venting. You're listening. That's what couples do."

Hudson scooped the spoon off the linoleum and tossed it back to her.

She caught it.

He clapped.

Giggling, she rolled her eyes.

Hudson drummed his fingers on the table. "It was only a suggestion." One he deeply regretted.

CHAPTER 4

From the comfort of her sofa, Mandie stared at the crackling fire through the woodstove's glass door. She still refused to put their wedding off until February.

"I think a Valentine's Day wedding would be more romantic." He shrugged. "Don't you?"

Mandie clenched her jaw, wanting to drop the subject and move on to something more fun. Like movies or books. "Valentine's? C'mon. Seriously. What a cliché."

"A cliché? Whatever." Hudson grunted. "Don't you think it would be more romantic than a Christmas wedding?"

Mandie tried to keep her voice peaceful with Nona on the floor now fiddling with a kitty puzzle and watching *Zootopia*. "Not as much as a December one." Like Holly, she'd always dreamed of being a December bride. Though she had already decorated her house with Nona's help, she didn't feel one speck of the holiday cheer at the moment.

And suddenly, she didn't want Hudson sitting next to her. Not wanting to be petty, she remained by his side. "I think we should keep the date. If for some reason I'm totally wiped out, which I'm not going to be, we can rethink things."

"Are you worried I'm going to get over there and not come back? I know you still struggle with abandonment issues and triggers."

"Kinda. I know you won't leave us. But still, the stupid triggers keep happening, and I'm afraid to let down my wall of protection."

"But your counselor said you might still have troubles for a while." Hudson held her hand. "Honey, I'm not going to leave you. Ever." He nodded to Nona, keeping his voice low. "I'm not someone's dad. Not a past boyfriend. Not your favorite uncle who died when you were nine. I plan on sticking around."

"I know. My head knows. But my heart . . ." She rested her head on his shoulder. "It's still hurting. I'm still struggling with the possible relocation too. Talk of changing our wedding date only adds to my anxiety."

"Okay, okay. No more talk of a change."

"Good. Because I want to marry you on New Year's Eve. Heck, I'd elope right now if my family wouldn't kill me for excluding them. I love you. You're the man I've always dreamed of. You're my anchor. My rock. I can't do life without you. I don't want to do life without you."

Hudson lifted her hand to his lips and kissed her fingers. "And I don't want to do life without you either."

"So no more talk of putting off our wedding?"

"None."

"For sure?"

He feigned a groan and grinned. "For sure."

"You two are talking crazy." Nona shook her head and went back to her puzzle.

"You're right. We are talking silly." Mandie gave Hudson a look.

"Enough crazy talk." Hudson let go of Mandie's hand. He draped his arm around her and pulled her close. "What's bothering you the most right now?"

His soothing touch sent warmth into her bones. She needed to snuggle her man. He looked extra handsome in his jeans, cowboy boots, and blue button-up shirt. She inhaled his woodsy scent. "I haven't heard back from Holly Sinclair yet. She's got me worried."

"Want to try calling her now? Maybe she had a busy day."

"I guess it wouldn't hurt." Mandie rose and fetched her cell phone out of her purse. She snagged the file from her tote bag by the door and made the call. "C'mon, answer." She paced the kitchen. Turned to Hudson and shook her head. When the time came to leave a message, she said, "Hey, this is Mandie Sellers again. Give me a call so we can set up an appointment to meet. Talk soon." She ended the call and tossed her cell phone on the table. "If it were me, I would have contacted my event planner by now."

Hudson patted the spot beside him. "Maybe there was a family emergency. Or maybe somebody's sick. Maybe she's sick." He gasped. "Maybe she's in the hospital."

Mandie laughed at his attempt at hyperbole. So like him. "You're right. It's probably nothing. I bet she'll call me tomorrow."

Nona padded to the kitchen wearing her purple slippers. "Mommy, I'm hungry."

"What would you like to eat, love?"

Nona thought for a moment. "Popcorn."

Mandie regarded the wall clock. It was almost bedtime. "How about a fruit snack?"

Nona let loose an irritating whine. "But I want popcorn."

"It's too late for popcorn. It's a fruit snack or nothing."

Nona's bottom lip protruded. "Fine." She scowled at her mom.

Mandie fetched the snack packet from the cupboard, tore it open, and handed the treat to her daughter. "After you eat this, go brush your teeth and get ready for bed. I'll be in shortly to read you a story and say prayers."

"Thanks, Mommy." Nona returned to her spot on the floor and popped a fruity snack into her mouth.

Hudson again patted the space beside him. This time, Mandie settled herself next to him. "Is there anything else that you're having a hard time with?"

"Well, I still can only get four pencil trees. According to the notes, she wants a Winter Wonderland theme. If that's what the bride wants, it's my job to deliver."

Hudson palmed Mandie's leg. "Are we still going to Spokane Saturday to find more pencil trees?"

"I called every store I could think of that might have them. They're all out. Not of every tree, but of pencil trees because they don't order as many. There's not a high demand. Which I can't figure out. I think they're cool. So no. I don't think we'll go."

"Who wouldn't want a skinny tree to hold a handful of ornaments? Imagine that." He gave her a playful wink.

She chuckled and slapped his hand. "Did you know pencil trees are the new Rockefeller Norway spruce? Besides, they fit plenty of ornaments." She raised a brow. "And they fit nicely in corner spots. They're perfect."

"That's a funny name for a tree." Nona shoved another fruit snack into her mouth and shook the upturned package.

"It's a very funny name." Hudson gave Nona a thumbs-up.

Nona giggled and tossed her wrapper on the floor.

Mandie frowned. "All right, missy. Throw your garbage in the trash and go get ready for bed."

"Do I have to?"

"Yes, ma'am." Mandie clapped her hands twice. "Get a move on."

"That's what the wranglers say to cows. I'm not a cow."

"Listen to your mom, Nona," Hudson said with a firm tone. "Get ready for bed."

The five-year-old pushed to her feet and dragged herself down the hallway.

Mandie appreciated him having her back. Raising a child alone had been a challenge. Having a man around, one who was gentle yet firm, had been a lifeline.

Hudson turned to Mandie. "What if this Saturday I cut you down however many assorted sizes of trees you need for your Winter Wonderland?"

Mandie bobbed her head. "That may work. And what about our cake tasting? I called them and they can't change our appointment. So I'll be eating cake by myself." She couldn't help claiming her self-pity. Then cringed. *Great. I sound just like my daughter.*

Hudson shot her a defeated look. "I'm sorry, babe. I'm doing the best I can."

She wanted to say, "Are you?" but held her tongue. "I suppose we all are."

"Sorry for giving you a guilt trip. I am looking forward to marrying you."

"I forgive you. And I'm looking forward to marrying you too."

"I'm also looking forward to having as many kids as you'll allow. I love Nona and can't wait to produce siblings for her. Being the only child stank for me. There was rarely anyone to play with. And I hated being called spoiled all the time. It wasn't fun."

"I'm sorry you had to endure those comments." Mandie attempted to keep her tone light. "But really. You spoiled? Never." She patted his leg. "I also look forward to enlarging our family." *Maybe just not as large as he hoped for.*

There was only one way to get Mandie Sellers's attention and that was to speak her language. On his way home, Hudson stopped at Seven Tine and picked up the extra whiteboard and markers he'd seen in the storage room. One way or another, he'd get Mandie to see that this new job, whether they moved or he commuted, was a viable option to secure their financial future.

She'd been a trouper, yes, but he wanted—no, needed—her full support. For his peace of mind.

Ten minutes after he walked into his cold, dark, undecorated house, his cell phone chimed. He answered the call without looking to see who it was. "This is Hudson."

"Hey, babe, it's me." Mandie sounded remorseful. "I owe you an apology."

"What for?" Hudson crumpled paper and shoved it into the woodstove before adding kindling. He lit a fire. Fledgling flames spit and sparked before finally breaking loose into yellow and orange flames.

"I was so concerned about myself and my problems, I didn't even ask you how your day went."

Hudson set his phone on speaker. Shedding his coat, he laid it over a kitchen chair. "Actually, I had a horrible day. One of the main reasons I want to get out of my job and get a different one. One that doesn't involve divorce and foreclosure." He settled himself on his easy chair.

"I'm sorry. What happened?"

"Today I got handed a client whose farm is being threatened by foreclosure, thanks to a divorce. The ex-wife got half of the farm, which she deserves, but because of child support and alimony, he can't pay the bills. This is the part of the job I hate. I can't stand to see people lose their homes and their livelihoods."

"I can understand how hard your job can be. But you can't treat it as though you're the one who is causing their problems."

"No, but it's never fun being the bearer of bad news." Hudson rubbed the back of his neck.

"I suppose I wouldn't like it either."

"So now do you understand why I want a new job? A job where I can help people, like your people, by saving salmon. And to help save the environment and their habitat."

"Yes and no. I understand the pressure and the emotional aspect of cases like this. But I don't see why you can't start your own business and pick and choose your clients with similar work. You can help people save their ranches and farms."

"The problem with that is when someone starts their own business, it consumes them. Especially as that business gets off the ground. I'd never see you and Nona. That would be hard on our marriage. Especially a new marriage. Don't you think?"

Mandie released a ragged breath. "Yeah. I suppose so. But I think we'd get through it. I'm going to be busy with event planning. Besides, wouldn't a new job in a big firm in a big city be just as bad? At least we would be in the same household in the same town. Versus you working remotely and being gone most of the time, sleeping God knows where in a different town. I'd rather be in the same bed at night with the man I love."

"But is that enough? Because I don't think it is for me. Yes. I want us to be in the same town most of the time." Hudson rubbed his eyes. "In truth, I don't have the energy for this conversation tonight." He needed her to see the board of pros and cons he was about to create.

"I'm not trying to pick a fight or anything. I just want you to hear me out."

"I've heard you. Believe me. Just because I disagree with you doesn't mean I haven't been listening. Can we talk about this tomorrow?"

A long, awkward pause. "I suppose so."

Yep. The only way she would understand the importance of the job is by seeing everything laid out on a storyboard.

"Thanks, hon. See you tomorrow. Love you."

"Love you more."

"Love you most."

When the call ended, Hudson tossed his phone on the couch and set up the whiteboard. He took out a blue erasable marker. On the left side, he wrote *pros*, and on the right side, he wrote *cons*. Then made a line down the middle of the board.

With a red marker and under *pros*, he made three huge money symbols.

CHAPTER 5

Mandie stood and brushed off her jeans. She enjoyed the mix of wood smoke from the popping stove and cinnamon from a red candle by the easels. She had just finished organizing ornaments on a few round tables the ranch hands had set up for her, along with some chairs, decorations, and lights. Next on her list was to tape out where each tree would sit, which took her an hour.

Then by text, she let Hudson know Saturday would be way too soon to cut trees. Hopefully, he'd be able to do it the following weekend. That would give her all week to decorate for both weddings since hers would also be held in the loft. All she'd have to do is switch out flowers and table centerpieces to her wedding colors—maroon and white.

Footsteps clunked up the stairs, and Leena appeared in jeans, a white hat, and her green down jacket—a tall, leggy Native beauty. Her eyes sparkled, and she wore a bright smile. She held out her arms and rushed over to Mandie with an enormous hug. "I missed you so much."

"I missed you too." Mandie released her. "How was your flight?"

"Thankfully uneventful." Leena took off her coat and hung it over a chair.

Mandie motioned for them to sit at the closest round table. "How's college?"

Leena plopped down. "I love Trinity University, and I love Utah. I went snowboarding with a couple of my classmates.

We had a blast. I love the mountains. Love the area. Love everything about the state."

"Fabulous." Mandie's chest clenched. She hoped Leena wouldn't give up her plans to become a singer. "Would you want to live there?"

"Is it Nashville?"

Mandie's chest lightened. "I'm glad you're going to stick with music. You have such a beautiful voice. I'd hate to see you throw away God's gift."

"Never." Leena examined the loft. "Looks like you got your work cut out for you. What are the Xs on the floor for?"

Mandie checked her cell for Hudson's reply. Darn. Nothing yet. "The bride-to-be wants to get married in a Winter Wonderland, so I'm going to give it to her. Nothing says Winter Wonderland like—"

"Trees!" the girls said in unison and giggled.

"Are you ready to talk music?" Leena asked.

"I sure am."

"This is for you, right? Not the other bride."

"Correct. According to your mom's files, they decided on canned music since it's a last-minute venue and date change. The group they hired can't travel over the pass because they have a gig somewhere else. But they do have a DJ lined up."

"Sounds good." Leena glanced around the room. "Where's Hudson?"

Mandie considered the time on her cell phone. "He should be here any moment."

"Should we wait for him?"

"No. Let's go ahead and get started. He can catch up."

"Do you have a song you want to walk down the aisle to?"

Mandie pointed to her storyboard. The girls got up and went to the easels. On Mandie's was a photo of Russell Dickerson. "The song I want is 'Yours.'"

"I know that song. It's a popular one. And Hudson's okay with it?"

"I'm not sure. If he hates it, we can choose another one. But I think he'll approve." *Why wouldn't he? It's the perfect song by one of our favorite artists.*

Leena hummed the melody of "Yours," then asked, "What song do you want for your first dance?"

"'Making Memories of Us' by Keith Urban."

Leena nodded and smiled. "I love that song." The look on her face suggested she had a boyfriend. Or at least a young man who had ignited a wisp of affection in her heart. "Do you have a playlist?"

Mandie reached over and grabbed her wedding notebook. "I do." She pulled a document out of a sheet protector and handed it to Leena. "Everything's right here."

"Of course it is." Leena's eyes grew round as she perused the list. "You want me to play a hundred songs in, what, two to three hours?" She held the paper out to her side.

"No. I can't decide which ones will make the final cut. I love them all." Mandie slouched in the nearest chair. "How many songs should I have?"

Leena sat beside her. "Considering every song is three to four minutes, you can expect to hear fifteen to twenty songs in an hour. But I'll take a couple breaks. So no more than twenty-five."

"Twenty-five?" Mandie pushed out a sigh.

Leena handed the sheet back to Mandie. "Good luck knocking off seventy-five."

Mandie groaned as footsteps plodded up the staircase. Hudson appeared more handsome than ever, wearing his dark brown Stetson and packing a whiteboard and a silver-framed easel, a plastic grocery bag, and a surprised look across his face. He must have forgotten they were meeting with Leena. To give him the benefit of the doubt, she said,

"Good morning. You must have written your favorite songs on that easel. Huh?"

He gave her a red-faced smile. "This isn't song-related, but we'll get to it soon. After leaning the whiteboard and easel against the wall and setting the bag on the floor, he settled himself next to Mandie. "Sorry. I forgot we were picking songs today." He jiggled his leg.

Mandie caught him up to speed and handed him her song list. He agreed with the two wedding songs and paled at her list of one hundred.

"What's the matter?" Mandie played with her engagement ring.

Hudson set the document on the table. "This is quite the list."

"Do you have any songs you want to add to it?" Leena asked with a look of concern in her eyes.

Hudson peeled off his coat and hat. He laid the coat on the floor and set his Stetson on the table, crown down, and combed his sandy-brown hair with his fingers. "Yeah. I do." He retrieved his phone from the inside coat pocket and set the garment back on the floor. He swiped the screen. "I have my top twenty here." He tapped his cell and handed it to Mandie.

Oh, my. Her pulse raced. "These are the songs you want to play at our reception?"

"Well, yeah. Why not?"

Mandie handed the phone to Leena. "These are definitely not songs I would have picked."

Leena perused the list. "Like I told Mandie, you guys need to pick about twenty-five songs. I know most of the ones on Mandie's list. But these . . ." She shook her head. "I've never even heard of most of these. Where did you get them?"

"They're old pop songs from my teenage years. I guess I just figured they were oldies but goodies."

"Goodies?" Mandie laughed. But stopped when Hudson frowned at her.

"Well, what we can do"—Leena handed Hudson's phone back to him—"is focus on the song you guys want to walk down the aisle and dance to. We can figure out your playlist later. Whatever songs I don't know, I suppose we can play them off your cell phone or something." She looked at Hudson and shrugged.

"We'll figure something out." Mandie drummed her fingers on the table.

"We sure will." Hudson gazed into Mandie's eyes with a look of determination.

He stood and held out his hand. "Shall we test out the song we plan to dance to?"

Mandie loved the way he looked at her just then. It sent shivers down her spine, the kind that settled in her heart and warmed her bones. She placed her hand in his and rose to her feet. With a heart-tapping grin, he led her to an open spot near the glowing woodstove and held her close. They started to move even before Leena began to sing.

But when her voice wafted through the room, it sounded as though heaven had let loose an angel as her melodic tone filtered through the room.

"No matter where we live, I want to feel this way for the rest of my life." Mandie lay her head on Hudson's chest. She listened to the lyrics that caused her to let go of every worry and doubt. She could see them in a two-story house, watching the sun sink into amber hues on a warm summer evening while Nona played on a tire swing. Or snuggled next to the fireplace in the warmth of their cozy home on a cold winter morning.

He tightened his grip on her, leaned down, and whispered, "You will never know how much I love you. I can't wait to marry you. I can't wait to bring more life into our family."

His warm breath sent goosebumps shimmering across her neck. What a grand day that will be. She'd have to trust God to work everything out for their good. Especially the date.

Hudson did not want to let go of Mandie. Her vanilla lotion had become his favorite scent. He prayed God would lead, guide, and direct them to make the best decision for their future.

When Leena finished the song, he kept moving, not wanting the intimate moment to end. And apparently neither did Mandie because her head still rested on his chest. Her breaths came low and shallow.

But it was time to show her his chart. He hoped to put her at ease about the job offer. He released her and kissed her hand. "I think the song is perfect."

Her face beamed. "I'm glad you like it." Soft footfalls faded toward the loft stairs, snagging Hudson's attention. He clung to Mandie's hand. "Thanks, Leena."

She stopped and turned around. "Sorry for trying to sneak out, but I didn't want to ruin the moment."

"That's okay." Mandie let out a soft sigh. "I'll get back to you by Monday with the top twenty-five."

"Before that, if you pick some of Hudson's funky tunes." She waved. "I'll catch you guys later."

Hudson led Mandie over to a table near the spot where he planned to set up the easel and motioned for her to sit down.

She lowered herself into a chair. "I'm excited to see what you're about to show me."

His pulse kicked up several notches. "I'm excited to show you." He set up the easel and set the whiteboard on a ledge, but kept it turned backward. Then faced his fiancée. "I made a list of pros and cons of taking the job and either staying here or moving to Seattle."

Her face fell, and her voice turned defensive. "Oh. I thought this had to do with our wedding."

"I'm sorry it doesn't, but I think you'll like what I have to present to you."

She inhaled a deep breath and nodded. "I'm listening."

If only there were Christmas music playing in the background to cut the tension in the room. "If you don't mind, I'm going to start with the pros." He turned the easel around and pointed to the first one on the list, realizing by the look on her face that he should have erased the three red money symbols. Too late now. He plowed forward. "This job with the Seattle firm, as I've said before, will most definitely secure us financially."

The thin line on Mandie's face proved she was not impressed. But hey, she managed a slight smile and nod when he cleared his throat.

Hudson wiped his sweaty palms on the sides of his jeans. "I probably should not have started with the money symbols. I'll admit that. But you have to agree, our financial security is a priority."

In unison, she crossed her arms and legs and offered him a slight nod tied to a blank stare.

Okay. "Another reason under the *pros* is there'd be a lot of opportunities for you and your event planning business." He let the idea of her owning a business sink in. To his dismay, her expression did not change. It did not lighten. It did not brighten.

"Nona would have a chance at a private school, a Christian school, a safe environment where she could—would—thrive. One that highlights God's biblical principles."

Mandie's posture shifted enough to offer a morsel of hope. But her legs and arms remained crossed. Somewhat deflated, he kept going.

"You would have convenience right at your fingertips. Grocery stores, shopping malls, movie theaters, bowling alleys." He added excitement to his tone. "Musical theaters and concerts. You wouldn't have the expense of travel, fuel, hotels, or expensive, overpriced meals."

A tiny spark of interest lit her face.

Hudson continued down the list, feeling every ounce of enthusiasm drain out of him. What was the point of addressing the *cons* if he couldn't even ignite excitement from a single *pro*?

Mandie's cell phone went off, and she scrambled for it two tables away. "Hello, Holly. It's good to hear from you." She held her index finger up to Hudson.

He nodded. Too bad he didn't get the same reaction to his presentation as the bride-to-be got.

"You were in the hospital with the flu and dehydration?" Mandie glanced at Hudson with a look of surprise. "Oh, I'm so sorry." She shrugged at him.

He gave her a small wave, promising not to tell her "I told you so." He also understood that she needed to talk to Holly. He sank into a chair and waited. Tried to figure out a way to get her excited about the Seattle job.

"Oh, I bet you're wiped out. Okay, I understand. You can meet when? Wednesday. Okay. It will have to be in the morning. I have another appointment in the afternoon." Mandie shot Hudson a sullen look.

Oh, how he wished he could have gone to Seattle on a different day.

"I see. Okay. Yes. Winter Wonderland. Okay. I understand. We can talk then. All right. Thank you for getting back to me. Take care."

Mandie moved back to Hudson and sat down. She clunked her cell phone on the table. "I can't believe she was in the hospital."

"How's she doing?"

"She sounds pretty rough. They gave her IV fluids, but she's doing all right. She's still not feeling well. At all."

"But you're going to meet on Wednesday?"

"Yeah, we are."

Hudson hoped that between cake tasting and meeting with Holly, Mandie would be too busy to meditate on his absence.

"Give me a moment, please." Mandie pushed to her feet, walked over to Holly's whiteboard, and added the date and time she planned to meet with her. When done, she set the marker on the ledge and turned to Hudson. "I take it you didn't get my text telling you this Saturday would be too soon to cut down the trees. I don't want them to get dried out. Can you possibly help me cut them down the following Saturday? That will give me a week to decorate them."

"No, I didn't check before I came to the loft." He added the date to his calendar. "Is a week going to be enough time?"

"If everything goes right, it'll be plenty of time." She lifted her finger. "Oh, I need a lot more decorations too. Holly has most of them. All I need to do is add some finishing touches."

"Great." Now, if there was nothing else his darling fiancée needed for the weddings, Hudson had to finish his speech before he lost her attention completely. After waiting a few seconds, he ditched the rest of the cons and pitched one final pro for moving to Seattle in his closing argument, hoping she'd like it or at least agree with parts of it, then fidgeted. "So tell me, and please be honest, what did you think of my presentation?"

CHAPTER 6

What did she think of his presentation? *"Be honest."* Really? How would he handle the truth? Mandie sat beside Hudson in the small country church at Grand Coulee Dam, located twenty minutes down the Columbia River from Nespelem. Her answer to Hudson reeled in her mind as they sat in a padded pew.

I think your presentation has valid points, but I'm just not a city girl. Would it be nice to have everything at our fingertips? Yes, it would. Would it be nice to have Nona in a private school surrounded by God's family? Absolutely. But at what cost? We'd have to leave our family, and Nona would grow up not knowing them as well. Plus, she would not be infused with her Native roots.

The pastor's commanding yet compassionate voice caught Mandie's attention.

He stood behind a pine pulpit with three crosses engraved in the wood. "Trying to control one's life only leads to disaster. Beloved, not trusting God leads to stress and anxiety. That lack of trust also tends to trickle down to family members."

Mandie couldn't argue with what he was trying to get across to them. Nona was like a sponge, picking up every morsel she said and reacting to it in her five-year-old way. Thank goodness she was with the other children rehearsing for the Christmas play, giving Mandie time to reflect and pray.

Her attention drifted to the stained glass cross perched behind the pastor. A faint light illuminated the colors. She felt her angst draining every ounce of her energy.

"Trust in the LORD with all your heart," the pastor droned on, "and do not lean on your own understanding. In all your ways acknowledge him, and he will make straight your paths."

How many times had Mandie read Proverbs 3:5–6? How many times had she given something to God and snatched it right back?

"When we surrender to God," the pastor said, "He gives us peace of mind, which reduces anxiety. You see, we have an opportunity for our Creator to work in our lives. When we surrender to Him, we have a chance to grow in faith and trust His plan. I challenge you today to free yourself from the burden of control and see what transpires. I think you'll be happy with the results."

Okay, God, this is me giving up my control to You. If You want me to move, then I guess I'm going to have to get in line with that. But please, Father God, make it crystal clear because You know my heart belongs here. You know my heart pleads for You to let me stay with my family and my people. Help Hudson not to be driven by money or what it can offer. Draw us both closer to You as we make this difficult decision.

They concluded the service by singing Brandon Lake's "Gratitude." As Mandie sang, God brought an awareness of her limitations, and at that moment, she surrendered everything to Him—Holly's and her weddings, Hudson and their careers, Nona, and a possible move. The knot in her tummy unwound as she lifted her hands and praised God.

In the fellowship hall, Mandie enjoyed cookies and coffee in to-go cups with Hudson and the others. Hudson picked gingerbread, and Mandie chose a peanut butter and chocolate chip mix. She took a bite and let the perfect balance of salt and chocolaty sweetness melt in her mouth.

Mandie finished her cookie and washed it down with strong black coffee. She turned to Hudson. "Can I talk to you?" When he peaked a brow, she added, "Privately."

With his mouth full of cookie, he nodded and finished his coffee.

They tossed their empty cups in the trash, wandered into the sanctuary, and sat in a pew.

"What's on your mind, babe?" Hudson bobbed his leg.

"God used today's message to speak to me this morning." She inhaled a deep breath. "I just want you to know that I've given over control to God. He has the reins, and He's in charge. Not me. I'm tired of being anxious and stressed. I haven't been trusting God. I haven't been trusting you to make the right decision for our family either. I apologize."

Hudson took her hand. "Pastor's sermon spoke to me too. And I know I need to stop letting the hook of money control me. I've always had it, and I guess I'm scared to not live comfortably. I'm scared that I won't be able to provide for you and Nona and whatever other kids we have in a way I'm used to."

"One thing I've learned growing up poor is that money doesn't make you happy. There's nothing wrong with having it. I just don't want it to rule us."

"You mean me. I make you happy, right?" Hudson gave her a playful smile.

Mandie gave him a sweet smile and tapped his shoulder with hers. "Yes. You make me happy." What she wanted to do was plant a passionate kiss on his tender lips. But this wasn't the time or the place. So she refrained. "And I do think your presentation had valid points. This country girl is trying to be on board."

"I know you're trying. And I appreciate it."

"In all honesty, I need you to consider Nona's heritage. She needs to be brought up in it. Needs to know her traditions. I want her to dance in pow-wows, representing her tribe. I want her to dance for God and to know her God-given Nimi'ipuu—Nez Perce—language."

"Wow. I never considered how important raising Nona here on the reservation is. You're right. I need to consider that, and I will."

Hudson let go of Mandie's hand and draped his arm around her. "Letting go is tough. I want to take the reins back. At the same time, I want to follow God because His will is so much better than ours."

"The struggle is real, that's for sure." She patted his knee. "I'm proud of your effort. I'm also thankful for your transparency."

The door creaked open and tiny footfalls ran toward them.

"I'm gonna be a sheep. Baahh." Nona stopped at their pew and climbed into Mandie's lap.

"You're going to be a fabulous sheep." Mandie squeezed her tightly, and Nona giggled. "I can't wait to see your play."

"I can't wait to see your play either." Hudson tickled Nona.

She giggled and buckled sideways. For a second, Nona's eyes glinted brighter. Then her little brows furrowed. "I'm hungry."

"Well then," Mandie said, "let's go home and get something to eat."

Hudson stood and put his arms out to Nona. She reached up for him. The gesture warmed Mandie's heart. She prayed their bond would continue to grow. And once again, she prayed it would be God's will for them to remain on the rez.

After lunch at Mandie's, Hudson drove home and banked the fading fire. Wanting to be comfortable, he changed out of his casual church clothes and into sweats. Then made a cup of coffee in his Keurig and added a spoonful of sugar and a trace of eggnog creamer. He took a sip and grabbed his phone before settling into his easy chair to call Mom.

Her voice sounded extra cheerful. "How are ya, son?"

"Good. Good. Yeah, everything's good." He pushed out a heavy breath.

"You said good three times. What's the matter?"

Do I tell her? "I presented pros and cons of taking a new job to Mandie."

"Perks of being a financial lawyer, I suppose. What was her reaction?"

"Not the reaction I'd hoped for."

"What was the first item on your list of pros?"

Unwanted pressure crushed his chest. "Three big red dollar signs."

Mom cackled. "That's something your father would have done. God rest his soul. But honey, that was your biggest mistake. I wish you would've conferred with me before you approached her. The way women reason is a lot different from men."

"I think I'm finally figuring that out."

"It's always best to start with what matters most to the woman. What does that look like for Mandie?"

"We were just talking about that after church. She wants to stay here. Being a Colville tribal member and raising Nona in her culture and traditions are super important to her."

"Seems I remember telling you this might happen not so long ago."

Hudson scrubbed his face with his hand. "I know, I know, but I had to get out of the city. Get away from . . . everything. I like the country. I like the open space and the laid-back pace. Riding horses and occasionally helping the hands with work. A long trail ride has become the stress relief I need."

"But?"

"I miss the ocean and options. Department stores. Concerts. Theater. Ball games. We either have to drive to Spokane or Seattle." He shook his head as a snippet of shame wound into his chest. "I even miss the money. That's what I struggle with most."

"Those are all valid reasons." Mom paused. "Did you mention the educational opportunities over here for Nona? We have private schools. Better ones, I'm sure."

"I did. That was the one thing that piqued her interest. But I don't think it's enough."

"You'll have to try harder. You would have never had these issues with—"

"Drop it, Mom."

"Just saying." She paused. "Anyhow, I think financial security lies on the west side, not on the east. You have a hard decision to make, son. I'll be praying you make the right one."

"Thanks."

"By the way, what were your cons?"

Hudson leaned his head back and closed his eyes. "Too many people. The rat race of travel. And the higher cost of living."

"I suppose one has to decide what they're willing to sacrifice for the success of their future."

Hudson sighed. He wasn't so sure he was willing to sacrifice Mandie's happiness and Nona's cultural roots.

CHAPTER 7

M andie had finally met with Holly this morning. It was Wednesday. Thank goodness they'd accomplished a lot. She sneaked to the kitchen, keeping away from the attorneys and their round of affirmations before they left. Late afternoon, a family reunion would roll in. She was glad to be away from the stuffy kitchen, cooking dinner for a group of twenty-seven, picky kids included.

After three hours of talking about decorations, budgets, and timelines, Mandie needed a break. Her brain was full. Happy but full. After grabbing a pumpkin spice muffin from the kitchen, she kicked off her clogs, bundled up, and wandered outside to the barn. Sun shone from the blue sky that filled the late morning with icy air. Holly was still not feeling the best, but her joy at Mandie's work gave Mandie a spring in her step.

Eleven working days until Vow Day. She shivered from the thought and the cold.

Inside the barn, where it was a few degrees warmer, she found her favorite horse's stall. It belonged to Sydney's blue roan mare. The horse poked her head over the Dutch door and nuzzled the side of Mandie's face. Mandie giggled, cupped her hands around Cyan's soft muzzle, and kissed her velvety nose.

"I'm happy to see you too." She inhaled the earthy scent and blew out her troubles over Hudson flying to Seattle. If only he truly understood how she felt. Cyan nuzzled her forehead against Mandie's chest as if consoling her. "You're such a good girl." With both hands, Mandie stroked the sides of the mare's neck and offered a short prayer. *I'm trying to let go.* She sighed. *I could use a little help.*

Parker, the ranch's colt starter, entered the barn and greeted Mandie with a nod and a smile. He ambled into the heated tack room. Though Mandie missed watching Chad Davis work with the young horses, she thought his replacement was doing a fine job with the colts. Minutes later, he came out with a halter and a coiled rope and fetched one of the three-year-olds he'd been working with.

"How's he doing?" She admired the bay roan stud colt.

"He's coming along nicely. I'm happy with his progress." He led the colt out the east sliding door and swung a left.

In the toasty tack room, Mandie found a bin of horse treats, filled up her pockets, and fed the remaining seven horses. After giving Sydney's mare one last neck rub and an extra treat, she wandered outside to the area north of the barn. Parker had the colt circling the edge of the round pen in a nice steady lope. The colt's inside ear flicked back and forth as he kept his attention on the wrangler.

Appreciating the bay's quiet eyes, Mandie moved closer to the round pen and tucked her gloved hands inside her coat pockets. As she watched Parker work the stud colt against a snow-covered, pine-covered craggy backdrop, she felt an unexpected twinge of reverence. She wanted the same type of relationship with Hudson. One of give and take. Trust. A deeper bond.

Would moving to Seattle put a strain on them as newlyweds? Was the move to event planning the right one? Is it what she truly wanted? Was she an event planner, or was she a daughter of God? Could she be both?

When Parker asked the colt to face him by stepping backward and looking at the ground, the horse spun inward, licking his lips. The bay trotted over to the wrangler in a posture of respect and gratitude. It was the same trust pair figure skaters had with each other. The kind she prayed she would have with Hudson.

If only she had peace concerning the move and her job shift. Did she want to be an event planner for Seven Tine? Should she branch out and strike out on her own in unfamiliar territory? Or did she want the safety and security that came with being an employee? There were too many risky variables. Especially with a child.

If she did move to Seattle, would she have the courage to break in as an unknown? Would she need further education? Or would she want to stay home with Nona? And volunteer at her school?

She sighed. *Lord, speak to me. What's Your will?*

She loved the ranch. Loved working for Sydney. And her heart told her to remain at Seven Tine. Even if it was only for one wedding. She intended to make Holly feel like the most precious bride in the world.

She would have to leave the rest to God.

Mandie's cell alarm reminded her it was time to taste cake. She jumped into her Highlander and turned up the heat. Half an hour later, she pulled up to Coulee Dam Cakes and More. Inside the toasty bakery scented with cinnamon and ginger, Christmas music played softly in the background, and a Christmas tree hovered in the corner.

She shed her winter garments and found the owner, a spunky blonde named Tillie who wore a red apron dotted with Christmas cupcakes.

"Not sure if you'd make it with the storm brewing and all." Tillie wagged her finger at the front windows. "I'm sure glad you did."

"There's a storm coming?" She should have kept an eye on the weather. Her mind whirled with what-ifs. What if the storm blocked the pass? What if Holly decided to cancel her wedding because her family couldn't make it in time? What if—she rubbed her temples, capturing her fearful thoughts and handing them over to God.

"That's what the news said." She flashed Mandie a festive smile. "All righty then. Why don't you take a seat, and I'll get your samples."

Mandie chose a spot by the window. A small, round, ornate vase filled with red-and-green ornaments and topped with red curling ribbon and green holiday picks centered the table.

Tillie brought out a tray of cake samples with maroon-and-champagne-colored frosting. Ah, her wedding colors looked lovely as a dessert.

Her mood instantly brightened. "These are beautiful. I can't wait to taste them."

The bell hanging over the door jingled, and a forty-something woman walked in. Tillie glanced at the woman, and then back to Mandie. "Let me know if you need anything. Otherwise, I'll check on you in a bit."

Mandie nodded and perused the choices in front of her. Tillie had labeled them with cute Christmas stocking markers. Mandie tried the vanilla confetti cake and raspberry lemon first. "Mmm." Tasty. But neither flavor spoke of nuptials. She went on to the spiced apple and almond amaretto. Both were a step up from the first two. But without Hudson by her side, neither flavor hit the mark.

Next, she tried the tiramisu sample and let the coffee and rum flavors roll around in her mouth. So far, that was her favorite choice. And Hudson more than likely would love the coffee in it. But honestly, without him, she couldn't choose.

The Christmas spirit had fizzled that morning when he said goodbye before heading to the airport. And so far, it hadn't returned.

Hudson stared at the cancellation notice on the flight information display board at the Spokane International Airport.

Could this be a sign that God did not want him to move? He rolled his suitcase over to an airline check-in counter and got in line where a woman in a United uniform stood at a computer. Her eyes looked frantic, but she remained calm.

When Hudson's turn came, he moved to the counter. "Is there going to be another flight later?"

She shook her head, clicking the keyboard with her long, silver fingernails. "It doesn't look like it. There's a nasty storm over Snoqualmie, and it's headed this way."

Hudson thanked her and moved aside to call Mr. Randall. He groaned when it went to voicemail. "Hey, this is Hudson Piccolo. I'm at the airport and my flight's been canceled. There are no flights out for the rest of the day due to a storm over the pass. Let me know what you'd like to do. For now, I'll head home. Take care."

The funny thing was, Hudson did not feel disappointed. In fact, he couldn't wait to get back to Mandie. He trekked across the road to the parking garage, jumped in his truck, and headed home. A light snow fell as he drove through Airway Heights.

On the drive back, he took in the beauty of smooth, white fields that had been filled with wheat and canola during the summer months. Was moving back to the city really what he wanted? Would he miss the open skies and amazing horizons? Miss the beauty of the desert, mountains, lakes, and streams on the Colville Reservation?

Would he want to replace helping farmers and ranchers and watching Mandie and Nona's excitement at the annual Omak Stampede and Indian Encampment with concrete and skyscrapers? Did he want to take the joy of the Native culture and traditions away from the two girls he loved the most?

He had to admit, there was something special about living in a small community in rural America. In a community he'd come to care about. And maybe that's why he was so frustrated. Because the care and concern for the people on the reservation and in Omak ran deep in his soul.

All he could do for now was wait to hear back from Gunner Randall. For some reason, he still felt led to go to the interview. If only he knew why. But God knew. So he'd go to the interview, learn about the law firm, and then he and Mandie could pray about it and see where God planned to lead them.

Two and a half hours later, Hudson pulled into Seven Tine and parked by the hay barn. He jumped out of his truck and jogged up the steps, finding Mandie in the midst of organizing ribbon, tags, and miniature snow globes on three added round tables. "Mary Did You Know" sung by Pentatonix blared through her cell phone. She looked beautiful in her skinny jeans, slippers, and a black sweater with gold round ornaments on it.

"Hey there, beautiful." Hudson wove through the tables and several strings of lights on the floor.

Mandie spun her head toward him, and her face exploded into a mix of surprise and joy. She jumped to her feet and met him halfway. "What are you doing here?"

Hudson kissed her luscious lips once. Then twice. "Of all things, my flight got canceled."

"No way." She squeezed him tighter. "Maybe it's a sign."

He chuckled but wasn't about to admit he'd had the same inclination. Not yet anyhow. "I tried to call Mr. Randall, but he didn't answer, so I came back. I'm not sure if he'll reschedule right away or not." He let her go. "Did you taste the cake?"

"I did, but . . ."

"But what? You didn't like any of them."

"The samples were fine. And in all honesty, it was hard to choose without you." Her gaze dropped to the floor. "Funny thing is, I didn't even want to be in control. We're a team. I want to taste cake and finish the playlist and every other detail with you because it's not my wedding, it's *our* wedding."

A knot formed in Hudson's stomach. "You're right. We should do this together. And I have time right now."

"That's sweet. Thank you." Mandie shifted her weight. "Unfortunately, Tillie doesn't have time to make new samples. That was our only chance. This being the holiday season, everyone's got their hands full. We're lucky we have Trey and his amazing photography skills as our wedding photographer and Leena's angelic voice, but everything else is. . . . Let me put it this way, we're on a timeline. A tight one at that."

It was obvious she was trying hard not to yank the reins out of God's hands. Way to go. Hudson was fortunate to be marrying this incredible woman. "What flavor was your favorite?" He sat her down at a table.

Her face brightened. "Tiramisu. You would love the mixture of coffee and rum. It literally melted in my mouth."

"Then let's go with that one."

She slouched. "I don't know if everyone else would like it. Around here, people like plain Jane chocolate and vanilla."

"Like you said, this isn't everybody's wedding. It's ours. And if that's the cake you want, that's the cake you get."

Mandie reached over the table and held his hand. "I know you're trying to be helpful, and I appreciate it. But how about we ask Tillie to make a two-tiered cake with one tier chocolate and one tier vanilla?"

"How about having three tiers and top it with tiramisu?" The smile on her face left him feeling lighter. He bent down to kiss her.

"Do you guys have the playlist?" Leena topped the staircase. "Oh, sorry to intrude." Her cheeks pinked as she crossed the room.

Hudson twisted around. "Oh, hey, Leena. No problem." He turned back to Mandie. "Shall we go over the list with her now and decide the top, what, fifteen?" He let go of her hand and put up his dukes. "I brought boxing gloves if we need them." He winked at her and dropped his arms.

Mandie giggled. "Yes, let's go with fifteen. I don't want to be here all night. We should get it done while we have you here." She fist-bumped him.

"Did you bring the sheet with you?" Mandie asked Leena. "If not, I've got an extra copy."

Leena reached into her coat pocket and pulled out a folded piece of paper. "Sure did."

She sat across from Mandie and Hudson.

"Great. I'll get mine." Mandie retrieved her copy from a box of supplies and rejoined them at the table. "All righty then. Let's mark some songs off our list."

"Yes," Hudson said. "So we can focus on Holly's stuff."

Mandie gave him a saucy smile. "That would be the best help ever."

"And you can choose all the songs." He tipped his head. "I only have one request."

A look of fear crossed Mandie's face. "What is it?"

"We play 'Rhythm Is a Dancer' by SNAP!." He gave her a sheepish grin.

"I don't even know that song." Mandie made a face.

Hudson hoped she wouldn't shoot down his only ask. "It's a late-'90s pop hit. C'mon, Mandie, you've really never heard it?"

"Never."

Leena pulled her cell phone out of her other coat pocket and tapped the screen. "Oh my gosh, I've played all the songs on your list, Mandie. But Hudson, I can't believe you listen to this stuff. You don't seem like the type." She found the song, and seconds later, the funky tune filled the loft.

Leena laughed and sang along. She shot to her feet and twirled and danced.

Mandie groaned. "You've got to be kidding me."

Hudson pulled Mandie to her feet and twirled her around, monitoring the tables so they wouldn't bump into one of them. Then they danced in place, away from anything that could break. "I would never kid about music." All three of them laughed and danced.

Until Hudson's phone vibrated in his back pocket. He let go of Mandie and retrieved his cell. The name on the screen cinched a knot in his stomach. An unexpected response.

CHAPTER 8

At seven the following morning, Hudson sat at his kitchen table with a cup of coffee, the taste of eggs, bacon, and toast lingering in his mouth. He listened again to the recording from Gunner Randall.

"I got your message. My secretary booked you another flight for the twenty-first. I rearranged my schedule so we could meet. I'll see you then. If you have any questions, give me a call. I hope you're enjoying the gift basket."

The basket he'd found on his doorstep when he'd gotten home last night, courtesy of UPS. He was glad he'd ignored yesterday's call and finished dancing with Mandie, faking a good time, after he'd seen who had called. The knot in his stomach had come back. How would Mandie react to the news? He dreaded telling her. But the sooner the better. Preferably today, because he wanted to be honest and open.

Hudson set his phone on the table, next to the cellophane-cocooned basket. He opened the wrapping and pulled out a bottle of red wine; two tall, stemmed glasses; cheese; crackers; canned salmon; gingerbread cookies; and chocolate.

He pulled a note from between the cheese and crackers and opened it. *Merry Christmas to you and yours.* It was signed *GR.*

How odd for them to send him a gift basket when he wasn't an official employee. Was this bait to hook him? Did they want him that badly? Or had Mom run interference once again, putting in a good word to various law firms to bring him home? Good grief. Had she sent the basket in Randall's name? He wouldn't put it past her.

He dialed Randall's number. It again went to voicemail. "Sorry to miss your call. I got the gift basket. Thanks. I appreciate it. And yes, I'll see you on the twenty-first." He ended the call and dialed his boss at the financial firm.

"Hey, my caseload is light. I need to help Mandie with the wedding plans. Do you mind if I take the day off?"

"Not at all. There's not much to do this time of year anyway."

"Great. I'll be in tomorrow." Hudson ended the call. Wait. He needed to run into Omak anyhow and grab more lights. He got Mandie on the phone. "Hey, babe. I'm taking the day off to come help you. Do you need anything other than lights?"

"You took the day off to help me?" Mandie sounded excited. "Oh my gosh. How sweet. I love it. Thank you. Hang on a minute. Let me check my list." Seconds later, she came back on. "Holly's coming in this morning. We're going to go over some things on her to-do list."

"She must be feeling better."

"She sounds better." The click of her boots on the wooden loft floor came through the line. "All right, here's my list. Eggs, milk, cereal. Please find a kind for Nona without a ton of sugar. Bread, sugar, molasses. Oh, and Sydney's auntie needs maroon ribbon to finish Nona's flower girl dress."

Huh? "You trust me to pick out . . . maroon?"

"I'll text you an image of the color. If you're not sure which one to choose, pick out the three closest. I can always take the other two back."

"Will do. I'll see you in a few hours. Love you."

"Love you more."

"Love you most." Hudson banked the woodstove, bundled up, and headed to Omak.

Around ten thirty in the morning, he dropped the groceries off at Mandie's and brought the lights to the hayloft. Since she was still with Holly, he set them down quietly and made his way to the guest ranch. Cinnamon, cloves, and baked apples filled the inside of the warm great room. To his left, a group of newcomers were full-swing in a game of Pictionary.

Hudson slipped into the kitchen where country music played over someone's cell phone that rested on a counter along with all kinds of snow globes.

"Hey, handsome. How ya doin'?" Shirley asked. "Have you met Paula Warden yet?"

"I have not." The women were elbow-deep in pie crust and fruity fillings from the island and the shiny, new commercial stove.

"It's a pleasure to meet you." Paula gave him a blissful grin.

"Likewise."

Paula set a ball of crust on a circle of flour and worked to flatten it.

"You two look busier than usual."

Shirley filled one of the pie crusts with baked apples hot off the burner. "Holly's bridal party is expected to come in next Wednesday. So is the groom's. We're trying to get ahead of the game since we're both taking time off for Christmas." She set the pot on the counter and examined her work. "What can I do you for?"

"I want to grab a snack and coffee for Mandie. Knowing her, she probably skipped breakfast."

"She does tend to do that when she's in work mode, doesn't she?" Shirley nodded to the counter between the batwing doors. "Help yourself to the leftover blueberry scones. There's a fresh pot of coffee at the bar. Pumpkin spice creamer's in the fridge. You can leave it out for the guests." She plopped a blob of crust on the counter and started rolling.

"You're the best." Hudson wrapped two scones in paper towels, fetched two lidded to-go cups of steamy pumpkin-spiced coffee, and rushed back to the loft. He held a cup in the air as Holly drove past as a goodbye gesture.

In the loft, blue-and-white fake flowers and ribbon and pine branches added to the already jam-packed floor. And somebody, probably Trey and the ranch hands, had moved in several more round tables, two rectangular ones, and chairs, and had them lined against the walls.

Mandie greeted him with a quick kiss, tasting of mint.

"I come bearing gifts. He handed her a blueberry scone and her to-go cup of coffee.

She sniffed the blueberry scone. "Mmm. This smells delicious. Thank you. I haven't eaten anything yet."

"I figured not."

A small frown creased her forehead. "Oh no. Was Walmart out of lights?"

"Nope. I set them in the bag over there." He pointed toward the stairs.

"Perfect. And you got the rest of my list?"

"On the counter and in the fridge." Hudson took a bite of his scone and chewed slowly, letting the burst of blueberries tingle his mouth. "These are so good."

"I'll tell you, Miss Paula's one amazing addition to the kitchen." Mandie took a bite of her scone and washed it down with coffee. She held up the cup. "You're the best."

"How was your meeting with Holly?"

"It went well. We nailed down every detail. So now all we have to do is get to work. You being here sure is lightening my load. I'm no longer stressed about doing the two weddings. I'm not stressed about anything. Except for Holly's cake."

"I thought Shirley was going to make the cake."

"That was my hope. But unfortunately, they have a ton of pies to make for her family and reception before Shirley leaves to visit her family in Montana."

"What about Paula? Her scones have proved she can do the job and quite well at that." He took another bite.

"She, too, is wrapped up with the pies before she heads out to Arizona for the holidays. Neither will be back in time." Mandie sipped her coffee. "Looks like I'm going to have to make Holly's cake."

"I'm kinda jealous." He winked at her. "What about the cake lady at Coulee Dam?"

"She's slammed this time of year. I doubt she has time."

"Do you want me to call her?"

"Go ahead." Giggling, Mandie gave him Tillie's phone number.

He punched in the number and when she answered, he said, "Hey, Tillie, this is Hudson Piccolo. Is there any chance you could bake another wedding cake?"

"Sorry, Mr. Piccolo, but my schedule is filled to the brim and overflowing."

He frowned. "I understand."

Mandie placed a strand of lights on the floor several yards away.

"I could pay double." He nodded to Mandie and smiled when she gave him a cheerful nod.

"I'm not sure you understand."

"Triple."

Mandie placed more lights on the floor, a few feet apart.

Tillie laughed. "I love your enthusiasm and your offer, but this is the holiday season. I'm swamped."

"Okay, but—"

"Sorry, Mr. Piccolo. I need to go. Best wishes to you."

"Right. Thank you so much."

Mandie gave him a victory laugh. "Told you so." She arranged lights across from the ones she'd previously placed on the floor.

Hudson helped her. "We'll figure something out."

"Done. I'll be baking the cake." Mandie shrugged, holding her hands in the air, palms up.

He gave her a look before turning to the corkboards. "What's on today's agenda?" He sipped his coffee, thankful the caffeine was kicking in.

"First, let's arrange the tables. After that, we can hang the lights."

Hudson set his cup on a table. "I'll fetch the ladder."

Mandie hooked his arm as he turned to walk away. "I got you something."

"Oh?" He pulled her into his arms and kissed the crown of her head. "What could it be?"

"I was thinking of giving it to you for Christmas. But ..."

"But what?" He bent to kiss her, but she put a finger to his mouth and stopped him. He groaned.

"You've been so helpful. And kind. And caring." She pulled him into a sway.

"Yeah?"

"So I got to thinking."

He swooped in for a kiss. "I'd love to know what's on your mind."

Mandie patted his chest and shook her head. "You've been such a good boy, you deserve a reward."

"I love rewards." He couldn't imagine what the gift could be.

She pulled a thin envelope from her back pocket and held it in the air.

Hudson stopped swaying and took the envelope. "What's this?"

"Open it." Mandie still couldn't believe Hudson took the day off to help her. What a gem. She shot him a sassy smile. The word *fortunate* to marry this man didn't even skim the surface of how she felt about him. And Nona was privileged to have him as a father.

Hudson slipped a Longhorn Barbecue gift card from the envelope. "Oh, wow. Aren't you a sweetheart?" He kissed the tip of her nose.

"I'm glad you like it." She settled into his embrace for a long moment. "It's the least I can do for all your help." Not wanting to leave the warmth of his arms, she broke away and fetched her cell from a table and put on Christmas music. "You ready to work?"

"I sure am." After stowing the gift card in the inside pocket of his jacket, he found a ladder, placed it where instructed, and climbed up. Mandie handed him a string of lights. He held them over his head. "How does this look?"

She stepped back, her hands on her hips, and took in the multibeam ceiling. "Yes, I think that will do. Now that we have them all lined out, we can crisscross them from beam to beam."

"Sounds like a plan."

"I'll hand them to you." Mandie loved how they were clicking today. Not as individuals but as partners. Like Parker and the colt. And with Hudson's help, she didn't worry about having only ten days left before Holly's wedding. With his help, she could easily pull off two weddings taking place within the span of one week.

"Sounds like a plan."

"With the lights up," Mandie said, "it's going to be easy to decorate the rest of the loft. And it will be simple to tear down her wedding colors and decorations and replace them with ours."

"Especially with the Seven Tine family and your family helping." Hudson secured the end of the lights on a hook, then climbed down the ladder and moved it to the next beam and set of lights.

Mandie handed him the end of another string. "Too bad your family's not arriving until the day before."

"That's okay. We have plenty of time to be with them." He climbed up the ladder.

More so if we move to Seattle. Oh, how her heart ripped in two over the possibility of moving. Mandie gripped the ladder as Hudson hooked the end. "And this is why you're going to make an amazing event planner."

"What's going to make me an amazing event planner?"

He nodded to the string of lights dangling from one side of the beams to the floor. "Moving from one side to the other. Then all we have to do is scoot the ladder to the other side of the room and work our way down to hang up the other ends. You're a genius." Hudson scooted down the ladder and cupped her arm.

Mandie's heart fluttered. "You're so sweet." She ran a finger across his stubbly jawline.

"I would have done one set and crisscrossed the room with this ladder." Hudson lifted her hand to his lips and pressed a kiss against her skin.

Her soul tingled. "No, you're a lawyer. You would have figured it out quick enough."

They finished up the lights, moved the rest of the guest tables to where Mandie wanted them, and after a quick lunch that included turkey sandwiches and chips, they set up the rectangular wedding party tables on one end of the loft and the arbor on the other end, where the ceremony would be held.

Mandie checked her cell phone. "I'd better go get Nona. Are you going to have dinner with us and hang out for a while?"

His brows pinched. "I would love to, but before you leave. I need to tell you something."

"Oh?" She crossed the room to Holly's whiteboard and checked off a few items. The tone of his voice suggested it might be something she didn't want to hear, so she kept her back to him.

"I heard back from Mr. Randall."

She knew it. Darn. She capped the erasable marker. "About?"

"Flying over there to meet him and check out the firm."

Just when she'd hoped and prayed that maybe, just maybe, he had changed his mind. Her tummy knotted as she slowly spun and faced him.

Hudson's Adam's apple bobbed as he wore a look of guilt on his face.

"You rescheduled?"

"Yeah. Honestly, I didn't think that would happen until after the new year, but he rearranged his schedule. What was I supposed to do?"

Say no. She crossed her arms. "When did you find this out?"

"This morning." He blew out a deep breath. "That's the call I didn't take last night."

"I see." Mandie tossed the marker in a box stationed beside the whiteboard. "When are you going to fly out?"

"The twenty-first."

Mandie nodded. She felt a storm rolling across her face but held it at bay. "Okay then." She turned back to the board and stared at her storyboard of sketches—cake, dress, maroon-and-white flowers. The perfect New Year's Eve wedding to begin a new life, with a new husband, in a new year. She should be excited.

Hudson strode over and hugged her from behind. "I'm sorry I didn't tell you before, but when I showed up you were happy. I didn't know how you'd react with me going since I know how badly you want me to stay."

"That's fine. I promised to get over my control issues and be open to a move. And I'm going to keep my word. I could have asked about the call."

Hudson shook his head. "I should have said something right away." When Mandie didn't respond, he asked, "What's on the agenda for tomorrow?"

"Do you plan on taking another day off to help me?" She hoped so. She enjoyed their time together today.

"I need to do some paperwork in the morning, but I'd like to take the afternoon off and do something fun. You've been working hard, and I think you and I need the time together."

"I wish I could take time off and do something fun with you. But I need to keep working. Sorry." The sorrow in his eyes made her focus on her red socks. "But thanks."

CHAPTER 9

S aturday morning, eight working days before Vow Day, dawned with a sparkly two feet of fresh snow. "What Child Is This" drifted through Mandie's Bluetooth speaker and from her lips as she decorated the tenth Christmas tree in the hayloft. From the rafters, string lights glimmered a soft blue. The fireplace snapped and crackled as it kept the area warm. The place smelled like fresh pine. Yum.

"Are you sure you're going to need five more trees?" Hudson handed her a pale blue snowflake attached to a white ribbon.

One could never have too many trees. Mandie hung the ornament on one of the lush branches of a tree bookending the bridal party table and grinned. "Five more, babe."

"Where do you plan to put them?"

"I need one small tree on each side of the wedding party table, in front of the pencil trees; one on each side of the stairs; and one, over there." She pointed to a line of three trees edged against the east wall.

"How tall do you want them?"

"I need two of them three feet, um . . ." Mandie turned her face toward the stairs that led to the ground floor, "and two of them five feet, unless I decide to flank the entryway with pencil trees, that might look better." She visually swept the room, rearranging trees in her mind. "Yeah, five feet, I'll put those on the west wall, and the other one, a nice six-to-seven-footer in the corner." She gestured to the crook opposite the garland-covered staircase handrails. Yes, the rearrange would work nicely.

"Okay. I'll go cut you down five more." Hudson donned his coat and Danner winter boots and headed for the exit.

"Hey, babe, what do you want to do after lunch?" She gestured to Holly's storyboard.

Hudson stopped and turned with a smile on his face that melted her heart. "I have plans." He waggled his brows.

Mandie's heart sank. "I thought you were going to help me today."

"Remember, yesterday I said I'd help you in the morning." He slipped on his knitted hat. "And then, let me rephrase. I have a surprise for us."

"Us?"

"Me and you."

"What about Nona?"

"She's with Sunny today." He tugged on his work gloves.

With her little sister? Huh. What was he up to? She set her hand on her hip. "Hon, I need to work. You know how important this is to me."

"You need a break."

"I need to finish."

"We will. Quit fretting." He hightailed it for the stairs.

"What time?"

"Be ready about two."

"Be ready about two? Yeah, right," she muttered. She had one week to finish flocking fifteen tree tips white, decorate said trees, finalize Holly's music with the DJ, pick up and arrange the flowers, decorate the tables, bake the cake. Good Lord, why had she thought she could do it all?

Yet she was getting it done with Hudson's help. He'd kept his promise, and for that, she was thankful. Thankful enough she wanted to do something more to show her gratitude. She crossed the room and stood at the top of the stairs, scrutinizing her work. Shades of blue, white, and silver threaded every tree, beam, and chair cover. She imagined what the tables would look like once they were complete.

She prayed Sydney and Holly would approve.

Footsteps caused Mandie to spin a half circle and scoot backward. Leena hopped up the stairs with a thermos and a Christmassy plastic container.

"Shirley wanted me to make sure you're eating." Leena handed Mandie the container and followed her to one of the center tables where her cell rested. The song switched to "Have Yourself a Merry Little Christmas." Leena sang a verse as she poured two cups of hot cocoa and settled in a chair across from Mandie.

Mandie opened the container. "Muffins and bacon. Yum." This reminded her of all the times she'd brought Sydney snacks to make sure she'd eaten, especially after her folks passed away in the horrific car accident five years prior. "There's enough for five people in here. You want some?"

"I'll take a muffin. They're raspberry." Leena glanced around. "You've turned the loft into a magical place. The bride is going to love it."

"I hope so. Glad you like it." Mandie handed her a muffin. She added bacon to the middle of hers and took a bite. So good. She sighed and washed the food down with a sip of hot cocoa. "Holly's going to come by Monday to check it out. Then I have six days to finish everything else, plus tackle a few items on *my* wedding list."

Leena got up and went to the storyboards. "Looks like you have a lot checked off."

"I'm getting there."

"Do you need any help?"

Yes. She would. But . . . "This is your vacation. Your only job is to rest and have fun. Enjoy your family."

Leena grunted. "Lester's such a mama's boy. He takes up all the time and is sucking the fun out of everything."

"It's age-appropriate. Remember Nona back then?"

"She was easy compared to my brother."

"You have a point." Mandie finished her muffin and lidded the container. "I'll save the rest for Hudson."

"Where is he?"

"Chopping down five more trees." Mandie gave Leena a spirited grin.

Leena looked around. "You don't think you have enough?" She took a drink of her cocoa.

"One can never have enough trees for a country wedding, Winter Wonderland or not."

Two hours later, Leena was long gone, and Hudson and the ranch hands hoisted the remaining five trees into the loft. Mandie had the stands ready and pointed out where each one should go. Under Hudson's direction, they fixed the trees to the stands, leaving the tallest for the corner.

Mandie found a string of blue lights and took them over to the highest one. "You guys are the best." She thanked the wranglers and turned to Hudson. "Will you help me string this one?"

"That's why I'm here." Hudson took off his winterwear, dropped it on the floor along with his cell phone, crossed the room, and took the lights. "Where do you want me to start?"

"How big is this one? It looks taller than seven feet." Mandie fetched the plastic container and opened it. "These are from Shirley."

He dropped the lights onto a table and chose a muffin and three pieces of bacon. "It's a little bigger than seven, but it was the nicest one out there. The boys and I figured you deserved the best."

"It's perfect." Mandie set the container by her cell phone and retrieved a box of ornaments while Hudson wolfed down his food before he wound the lights around the tree.

When done, he plugged them in one set at a time. "I hope the barn doesn't burn down with all of these trees lit up."

"Trey assured me they wouldn't." Mandie laid out the ornaments on the closest round table. She chose two silver stars and handed one to Hudson. She went to hang hers on the tree she had when a click echoed through the loft, and the room went dark.

The "Silent Night" chorus drifted through the room. Awesome.

"I think Trey was optimistic." Hudson set his silver star ornament on the round table. "Do you have a flashlight?"

"This can't be happening." Mandie hung a star on one of the white-flocked tree branches. "To answer your question, I have one on my phone."

"Cell flashlights aren't bright enough. I'll go find Trey." Okay, so the smartphone would work. But he had to make sure the wranglers were hooking a horse to the sleigh for Mandie's surprise. Plus, he needed to find out where the electrical panel was. He slipped back into his winter wear and stomped down the stairs, finding Trey in the barn with his vet. "Hey, what's going on?"

Trey kept his attention on the blue roan stud colt. "Myrrh seems to have a bellyache."

"What from?" Hudson shoved his hands into his coat pockets, wishing he'd put on his gloves.

"We're not sure." Trey peered at Hudson. "How's the loft looking?"

"Dark."

Trey lifted his brows. "What do you mean 'dark'?"

"I plugged in tree number eleven and the power went off."

"Did you check the panel?"

"Not sure where it's at."

"It's to the right of the door. I need to stay here so you're on your own." Trey turned back to the horse.

"I'll check it out." Hudson went back to the hay barn and stepped inside the dark, alfalfa-scented space. Shoot. He'd left his cellphone in the loft. He trudged back to the horse barn.

"Did you find it?" Trey glanced at him, then turned his attention back to the young horse.

"I need a flashlight."

Trey motioned to the tack room. "You'll find one on the counter."

Hudson found the flashlight, went back to the electrical panel in the hay barn, and flipped the switch. Nothing. At least now Mandie couldn't fight him about going on a sleigh ride. He trudged back upstairs. "The power's not coming back on, and Trey's busy with a sick horse. So let's take a break, pray he gets the power on in a few hours, and go do something fun."

Mandie frowned. But a breath later, her eyes danced in the glow of the woodstove. "If you shine the light, I'll hang ornaments." She held one up.

Hudson flicked off the flashlight. "Sorry. Batteries are dead." He admired his fiancée's spunk through the shadows playing on her face.

"Very funny."

He took her hand and led her to the pile of coats and hats piled on the floor next to the staircase. "I have a surprise for you. Will you please get these on and come with me?"

Mandie tipped her head. "Only if you get a thermos of cocoa and find two travel mugs."

"Done." He hoped the wranglers were ready. "Stay here. I'll get the cocoa. And a treat." He handed her the flashlight.

"Good. I'm still hungry." She turned the light on. "I thought the batteries were dead."

"Oops. My bad." Outside, Hudson ensured the horse and sleigh were ready before going to the guest lodge.

Fifteen minutes later, he returned with two insulated mugs and a thermos. Mandie was hanging an ornament on the tree with the help of the flashlight beam. "You ready?"

"Let me do a few more." She plucked a snowflake ornament off the table.

Hudson crossed the room and took hold of the ornament. "Later." He set it back on the table and led her outside by threading his arm through hers.

In front of the horse barn stood a red-and-white sleigh hooked up to a red roan mare. Around the horse's neck was a big red bow and three large bells. The horse stood with the patience of an elder, as if knowing she was about to take two people on a romantic journey.

Mandie gasped and palmed her chest as she made her way to the horse's head. With both hands, she stroked her velvety muzzle. "Ah, Timpts." She referred to the Nez Perce name for the horse, meaning chokecherry. "You set this up for us?"

"I sure did." He enjoyed her reaction. "You've been working hard. You need a break."

"Does that mean you had something to do with the power going out?"

Hudson chuckled and put his hands up in surrender. "I swear I had nothing to do with the power going out, but I'm not sorry it did." He lowered his arms.

Mandie kissed him and hopped in the sleigh. A picnic basket sat on the floor. And on a Pendleton-covered bench in green tones rested a fluffy Christmas blanket, the two insulated mugs, and a green thermos. She climbed in and covered her lap with one half of the Christmas blanket and lifted the other half for her fiancé.

Hudson climbed in, sat next to her, and laid the blanket over his lap. After giving a nervous smile, he took hold of the reins and said a quick prayer, hoping to remember Parker's driving lessons. "You ready?"

"Are you sure you don't want me to drive? Syd taught me how a few years ago."

"Nope. I want you to sit back and relax. I can handle it."

"You sure? I've got skills." She flashed him a sassy grin.

"I'm sure." He flicked the reins over Chokecherry's back. The mare took off toward the north pasture in an easy walk, her hooves crunching the snow.

They glided past the cabin, past Trey's photography studio, and through a copse of pine trees that opened up into a carpet of white sparkling pastureland. Overhead, fluffy white clouds held in the day's meager heat. Snowbirds serenaded them, and minutes later, a buck with a full rack bounded across their path heading for Nespelem Creek.

"Thanks for your help today. I appreciate it." Mandie giggled. "I think Holly's going to like all the trees."

"Yeah, she is. The trees are perfect. I like the white stuff you tipped the trees with. They look frosty. The way you have them set up is pretty special." He wanted to hold her hand but didn't want to lose sight of the reins, being this was his first time out with Mandie. He didn't want to mess anything up.

She sank into the seat. "There's still so much to do, even for our wedding."

"A. You'll get through it. B. This is a no-work-talk date. I won't talk about my clients if you don't talk about the weddings."

"Not even ours?"

"No. Because it's tied to Holly's."

She patted the blanket covering her legs. "What should we talk about?"

"How about you peek in the picnic basket and maybe pour us some hot cocoa?"

"I can do that." Mandie tugged the gloves off her hands, unscrewed the thermos lid, and poured two cups of minty cocoa into the travel mugs. She handed one to Hudson. He took a sip and put the mug between his knees.

Mandie also took a sip of hers. "This is delicious. Thanks for adding the candy cane bits."

"I know it's your favorite." Hudson flinched when Chokecherry wagged her head, chiming the bells. He pushed out a sigh and relaxed when the mare settled back down. "Take a look in the picnic basket." Hudson tossed her a spirited smile.

Mandie opened the basket. "What is this?" She lifted out a maroon sweater with white snowflakes and reindeer on it. "This is beautiful. I love it. Thank you. What's the occasion?"

"I wanted to give you a little something for working so hard. Plus, I couldn't resist it because it's our wedding colors."

"I didn't know you could be so romantic." She leaned over and gave him a frosty kiss.

"My pleasure. Can't wait to see you in it." He gave her a sideways glance and a feisty smile.

"What else is in the basket?" He shot her a playful grin.

Mandie reached in and pulled out a container. She unlidded it and lifted the aluminum foil lining to reveal two sandy brown muffins. Cinnamon and ginger waltzed with the crisp air. "Don't tell me you made these." She studied him. "Did you?"

"I wish. Remember, I grew up with a hired cook in the house. My mom didn't even bake. So no, I did not make them, but I had help."

"Shirley?"

"I'll never reveal my sources."

Chokecherry halted near Nespelem Creek. The bubbling brook was frosting on the ride's cake. The current glittered in the sunlight. And pine and fir trees drooped with what looked like whipped cream. Hudson rested the reins over the front of the sleigh and took a sip of his hot cocoa. Mandie handed him a muffin.

"These smell delicious. The baker, whom I still will not mention," he said with a smile, "claims this is a new recipe." He took a bite. "Hmm."

Mandie dug in. "Oh my goodness. We need these for the wedding. Holly would love them. I need to call her." Mandie reached for her cell phone.

Hudson groaned. "You just can't stop thinking about work, can you?"

CHAPTER 10

The following Monday, late morning and six days before Holly's Vow Day, Mandie stood in the shadowy loft, wearing the sweater Hudson had given her, and chewed on her fingernails. Thank goodness the stove was wood and not pellet. At least they had a bit of a glow and heat. "When do you think you'll get the lights back on?" she asked Trey, who wore canvas coveralls and a jacket and was inspecting the outlet and electrical cords with his headlamp by the over six-foot tree.

"The electrician should be here any time." Trey gazed at her. "Why don't you go to the lodge, and I'll let you know when everything's fixed."

"You think an hour? Or two? What are we looking at?" With his headlamp aimed past Mandie, she squinted at her to-do lists. Good gracious. What else could go wrong? Without any lights, this would be the darkest Winter Wonderland ever.

Trey dropped the cords and turned his head, erasing her light. "I'm not sure. It might only take an hour, but there are no guarantees."

Mandie sighed then gathered a box containing her notebooks and Holly's party favors. Her cell phone rang. The time read 11 a.m., and the bright screen revealed Holly's DJ's name and number. Oh good. She welcomed his confirmation and appreciated his timeliness. She answered the call.

"Hey. I hate to do this, but I have to cancel working Holly's wedding. We have a family emergency."

Shock choked the air out of her. She blinked several times. Had she heard him correctly? "Oh-um-I'm sorry to hear that. I hope everything's okay."

"I do too. My dad had a stroke. Sounds like it's pretty bad. I need to fly back to New Mexico."

"I'm so sorry to hear about your dad and totally understand. I'll be praying for you and your family."

"Thanks. I appreciate it."

"Do you have a referral?" She moved to Holly's to-do list and shone a flashlight on the easel. Then she snatched a marker from a box on the floor and uncapped it.

"I called a few of my friends. Unfortunately, they're already booked or can't make it. I hope you can come up with something."

"Don't worry about it. Go be with your family." She capped the pen and tossed it back in the box.

"Thanks for understanding. I hope you have a merry Christmas."

"You too." Mandie ended the call and sank into a chair. She put her face in her hands and pushed out a squeal. There was no way she could find a replacement in six days. And this close to Christmas. But she had to try something before she called Holly.

"What's the matter?" Trey asked from the front trio of trees near the right side of the wedding party table.

Mandie squinted as the blinding light coming from Trey's forehead hit her square in the eyes. "We lost Holly's DJ. I don't know what to do. I don't want to call her until I try some of the musical people I know. Maybe somebody from church can fill in."

Trey shifted his head so the light wasn't shining in her face. "Why don't you go to the lodge office and make some calls? Or better yet, ask Leena."

The idea had popped into her mind as he voiced the suggestion. "Good idea. Is she around?"

"You can check. I think she went with Sydney to do some last-minute Christmas shopping. But they might be back by now."

"Perfect." Mandie grabbed the box. "Please text me as soon as we have power."

"Will do." Trey went back to inspecting electrical cords.

Mandie descended the stairs as a Silver Toyota Tacoma pulled in and parked by the hay barn. She nodded to the man inside and made her way to the lodge. Must be the electrician. Thank goodness.

Inside the lodge, a fresh round of guests for the family reunion either played cards or board games, worked on a puzzle, enjoyed a book by the fireplace, or perused the well-stocked gift shop. Mandie set her box on an unoccupied dining table. She fetched a steamy mug of pumpkin spice coffee and went into the kitchen to nab another one of those delicious gingerbread muffins from Saturday.

"Try one of these." Shirley handed her a decorated sugar cookie in the shape of Mrs. Claus.

Mandie took a bite, hoping for a little Christmas magic. "Mm." Chewing slowly, she found a gingerbread muffin in the fridge and warmed it in the microwave.

"Power still out in the hay barn?" Paula glanced up from decorating a snowman.

"Yep. And Holly's DJ just canceled due to a family emergency." She told Shirley what had transpired and sighed. "I'm going to do a little work from the office. I'll catch you guys later." She strode out of the doors. As they swung back and forth behind her, muffled voices piqued her curiosity. No.

She couldn't pay attention to what the cooks were talking about. She had a DJ to find. Unless Leena could pinch-hit. She wanted Holly's wedding to be exceptional. Having a live entertainer would make the wedding special.

Sydney and Glenda's laughter pinged from the office, so Mandie settled in a chair by her box of notebooks and party favors and texted Leena. With no reply, she enjoyed the rest of her cookie and started in on the muffin and half a cup of her coffee before calling her church's worship leader as a backup. "Hey, this is Mandie." She told her about the DJ's cancellation. "Do you think you or anyone at the church can fill in? It's a paying gig."

"You're talking this Saturday, right?"

"Right." Mandie chewed on her pinky nail.

"It's doubtful. But why don't you let me make a few phone calls, and I'll get back to you in a few days."

"If you can get back to me by tonight, that would be better."

"I'll see what I can do."

Mandie ended the call. "Help, help, help," she prayed. She set her phone on the table, finished the muffin, and fetched a cup of hot cider.

Seconds later, Sydney strode, not quite a waddle but getting there, out of her office and toward the coffee bar. "How's it going in here?" She picked out a Christmassy mug.

Mandie set the cell phone on the table. "It could be better."

Sydney poured a cup of cider and joined Mandie at the table. "Trey and the electrician should have the power on soon."

Mandie told her about Holly's music debacle, wishing she had another cookie to help take away her angst. But she didn't want to put on the extra pounds with her impending wedding. She'd already had more goodies these past few days than intended.

"Leena's been singing up a storm of Christmas songs and the songs from your wedding list. Right now she's at the retirement home in Nespelem making a bunch of elders very happy." Sydney blew on her cider and took a sip. "She might be able to help you out if Holly's not picky about her wedding and reception music."

"I haven't talked to her yet. I want to wait until after I hear from either Leena or my worship leader."

"I bet Leena will be happy to help. She was telling me the other day that she needs the practice to get more comfortable singing in front of a crowd. Between a few local gigs and Holly's and your weddings, she'd get in lots of practice."

"Good to know. Hopefully I'll hear back from her and my worship leader soon."

"All righty, well, I'd better get back to work. I'll be praying for you."

"I could use lots of them right now."

Sydney rose and went back to her office.

An hour later, Mandie was almost done creating and bagging Holly's miniature snow globe and candy wedding favors. All she'd needed to add on Vow Day was the blue-and-white frosted snowflake cookies and the couple's names and wedding date tags that were already threaded with a dark blue ribbon.

The lodge's door creaked open, and a gust of wind rolled in and swirled around Mandie's feet. Several seconds later, Trey strolled in wearing sheepskin moccasin slippers, jeans, and a black Seven Tine Guest Ranch–logoed sweatshirt. He plopped down beside Mandie, his cheeks rosy from the cold.

Sydney strolled out of the office. "I thought I heard my handsome husband come in." She joined them at the table, gave Trey a kiss, and settled into a chair next to him.

"I got good news and bad news," Trey said to Mandie. "What do you want first?"

"Oh, good grief. I'll take the bad news first."

"Actually, I'm going to give you the good news first."

"Which is?"

"We're getting an electrical upgrade in the hayloft to handle your copse of trees for your fancy Winter Wonderland event." He flashed her a peppy grin.

"Wedding."

"Whatever."

Mandie grunted. *Men.* "And the bad news?"

"They can't fix it till Friday."

Mandie swore her heart stopped. "Friday. You can't be serious. You're teasing, right?"

"Yes, I'm joking." Trey ducked when Mandie tossed a handful of leftover candy at him. "It'll be fixed Wednesday."

"You're horrible." She gave him an exasperated laugh.

"Come on now. I'm simply sharing a bit of holiday cheer. You've been way too serious this month, even though I know you're working hard to impress the boss." He tipped his head toward his wife. Sydney lifted a brow and pinned him with a disapproving look. "In all honesty, I miss the spunky Mandie. Do you think she'll come back anytime soon?"

"Oh, yeah. She'll come back the Sunday after Vow Day."

"I look forward to seeing her." Trey set his hands on the table. "Wait. That's Holly's wedding day, right?"

Mandie smiled and nodded. *Genius.* She threw more candy at him. This time, nearby kids scrambled to the floor, as though someone had cracked open a piñata, and scooped up handfuls of the sugary delights.

"That's mine!" a preschool boy said and snatched it from an older girl who wore green slippers.

Green Slippers stuck out her tongue and grabbed a different one. "Ha ha." She held up her treat and went for more.

In seconds, the kids had the floor clean and returned to their games.

"I have more good news if you want to hear it." Trey's cell phone chimed. He held up his index finger for her to wait a minute.

Leena entered the room through the batwing doors and sat down by her dad. She laid her head on his shoulder, looking flushed.

Oh no. Not Leena. *Please, Lord. Don't let her be sick.*

But the moment Mandie finished her prayer, Leena palmed her chest and let out one hack of a cough.

Hudson had just enjoyed one of his favorite meals. Mandie had created it in appreciation of his helping her. *What a treasure.* He rose, fetched a plate of cookies and milk, and joined her once again at the kitchen table. He'd set dessert next to a gift bag embossed with snowflakes. A few minutes ago, Nona had fallen asleep on the couch. A fire lit the window of the woodstove, and a cedar-scented green candle flickered in the center of the table.

Yeah. A romantic evening in was something Mandie and he needed. He picked up a cookie. "I'm glad Trey hooked you up with a generator and a few lights so you could keep working."

"That was a tremendous help. Though I'm still mad at him for teasing me about the power being out until Friday." She scrunched her face.

Hudson let out a small laugh. "I would be too. But it is kind of funny."

"Not really." Mandie chuckled as she lifted a cookie from the plate.

He gestured to the gift bag with his chin. "Are you going to open it?" All he wanted to do was offer his fiancée a bit of holiday joy.

"What's going on? First, this new sweater. And now, another gift? With 'Soon-to-be Mrs. Piccolo' on the tag?" She seemed to be half joking but half serious.

"Just open it, babe." He moved the bag closer to Mandie. "It's actually not from me."

"It's not?" She opened the bag and pulled out a maroon-and-white silk floral scarf. "This is gorgeous. Where did you find it? I'm sure you didn't find anything this wonderful around here. Did you order it online?"

"I told you, it's not from me. Read the card." He couldn't wait to see her reaction to Mom's thoughtful gift.

Mandie dipped her hand in the bag, pulled out a card, and opened it. "I look forward to having another woman around. I'm also looking forward to you two moving to Seattle." Mandie tossed the card on the table. "She thinks we're moving to Seattle? Does she think you've already accepted the job? What's going on, *Hudson?*"

He picked up the card and read it. "I don't know what she's doing." And he didn't like it either. "I keep telling her I don't know where we're going to live."

"Did you tell her I want to stay here? Did you tell her the decision is between *us?*"

"I've told her more than once." He dropped the card on the table. "She's persistent. It's the lawyer in her."

Mandie fingered the scarf. "It must have been hard living in the house with two attorneys."

"Listening to my parents talk about their cases was interesting. But my mom was never like this until my dad died. With me being the only child and her not having any family around Seattle, it's been hard on her."

Mandie twisted her engagement ring around her finger. "Listen, I love your mom. I really do. But she needs boundaries. I want her in my life—our life. I want her to get to know Nona. But . . ."

Hudson didn't like the look on her face.

"If she's always going to be in our business, and if she's always going to want to be the center of everything, I for sure don't want to move to Seattle."

How could he get Mom to stop trying to manipulate things? "I promise she won't come between us. Give me another chance to talk with her. Just give her time."

"How much time does one woman need?" Mandie sucked in a sharp breath and slumped in the chair. "Sorry. I just want us all to get along."

"I'll talk to her. Tell her to back off because you and Nona are my priority. And I'll let her know you want to include her and that we want her in our lives. And I'll be better at setting firm boundaries."

"Please do." Mandie softened her countenance. "Sorry for being snappy. Today's been a bit rough."

"Like I said before, if we need to put ours off—"

"We're not rescheduling our wedding. I can do both. Besides, I have to prove to Sydney I can handle the pressure. I need to get out of the kitchen."

"I thought you liked to cook."

"I love to cook. But I want to do more. And I can still do some of the baking if necessary. I'm sure Sydney will let me use the ranch kitchen since future bookings will be ranch events. And if she hires Paula on a permanent basis, that'll make life easier for everyone."

"I hate to see you stressed out."

"I hate to feel this way." Her gaze swept over her little girl, who was bundled in a fluffy white blanket on the couch. "If only I could feel as peaceful as Nona looks."

Hudson's cell chime caught his attention. Keeping his gaze on Mandie, he answered. "Hello."

"Hey, this is Gunner Randall. I have a slot open in my calendar for Wednesday at five. I'll have my secretary change the flight. We can talk over a nice lobster dinner. What do you say?"

"Wednesday, huh?" The defeated look on Mandie's face made him want to decline the lucrative offer. "I'll put it on my calendar."

"Great. See you then. I'm excited to show you my offer. You'll be impressed."

"I'm excited to see it, sir." Hudson ended the call and set his phone on the table, screen down.

"Was that Mr. Randall?" Mandie looked anything but thrilled.

"Yep."

"I take it you're going to Seattle. Wednesday."

Hudson nodded. He was starting to dislike that day of the week.

"For the job interview?"

"I'm going to hear him out. That's it. I want to know what my options are. We've already talked about this, Mandie. I'm not going to make you like it, but I do want you to be okay with me going."

This time Mandie's cell rang. Her face lit up as she grinned at Hudson. "Hey, is anyone available?" Her countenance dimmed. "No? Well, thanks for trying." She set her cell on the table. "That was my worship leader. Neither she nor anyone else is available. Leena's sick. What am I going to do?"

The tears that threatened to drip from Mandie's beautiful brown eyes stabbed at his heart. He wanted to volunteer to help, but knew nothing about DJing.

CHAPTER 11

T hank the Lord. The power stayed on all day. At two in the afternoon on Wednesday, Mandie finished attaching blue fairy lights to silver spray-painted boughs used for the centerpieces. All she had to do now was spray paint the glass vases silver and insert them with two-toned blue floral sprays. She plugged in the tree and overhead lights, kept the fairy lights on, and flipped off the switch at the top of the staircase.

The loft truly resembled a winter wonderland. Taking it all in, she pressed her fingers to her mouth, wishing Christmas Eve was her wedding day.

"Oh my goodness, this is gorgeous." Sydney's voice came from behind her.

Mandie startled and flipped around. She pressed a hand to her chest. "You scared me half to death." How had she not heard her boss tromping up the stairs?

"Sorry, I didn't mean to surprise you." Sydney palmed Mandie's back.

"That's okay."

"You have done a fantastic job. Holly's going to love this place."

Mandie faced the room, her pulse rate lowering. "I'm glad you like it." But was it good enough to earn the event planner title?

"I wanted to let you know Leena's going to the doctor today. Between the natural medicines my aunties have given her and what the doctor prescribes, she should be fine to sing for your wedding. Maybe for Holly's too."

Mandie's pulse raced again. This time due to joy and thanksgiving. "Thanks for letting me know. If all else fails, we'll go with the original plan and play canned music for Holly's ceremony and reception. If needed, Hudson and I can do the same." She'd be disappointed, though. She rubbed her right temple.

"Don't worry about what you don't have control of." The woman put a gentle hand on her arm. "Canned music is better than none. And this is about their vows to each other in front of God. Weddings aren't about the reception or the music. They aren't even about this beautiful space. They're about the commitment. Everything else is extra."

"Thanks for the reminder."

"I need you to take a break. I have something to talk to you about in my office concerning the new ranch cook."

The look on Sydney's face caused Mandie to stiffen and her belly to flop. Was Paula not working out after all? But she thought Sydney liked her. Why in her office? Mandie flipped the loft lights back on. "Let me do a few more things, and I'll come over."

"I'll wait for you. Once you get started on something, you tend to lose track of time." Sydney gave her a lively smile.

"At least let me unplug all the lights."

"I'll tackle the fairy lights if you want to get the trees."

"Deal."

Minutes later, Mandie stomped her feet to get the snow off before she entered the guest ranch. Inside, she took off her winter clothing and inserted her feet into her clogs, expecting to hear something about the event planning job. Or perhaps Holly's wedding.

She stepped into the great room, her mind still whirling.

"Surprise!" Dressed in Christmas sweaters, Trey, Rita and Robert Elliot, Chad and Sophie Davis, Sydney's aunties, Mandie's mom and sisters, her three aunts, a handful of her closest friends, cousins, and Nona clapped.

Nona ran up to Mandie and raised her little hands above her head. Mandie giggled and picked up her daughter before addressing the crowd. "What are you guys doing here?" She loved their sweaters, worn in honor of her love of Christmas sweaters, no doubt. Sydney took off her coat, revealing a maternity sweater that matched Trey's.

"We took a week off," Rita said, "to come here and have Christmas with everyone and our families. And to have this surprise bridal shower for you, Miss Wedding Planner." She winked at Mandie. "None of us is going to miss your wedding, girl." She gestured to her, Robert, Rita, Sophie, and Chad.

"Because you've always taken care of us." Sydney gave Mandie a sweet grin.

Hot tears stung Mandie's eyes, and she blinked them away. She greeted everyone in the room with hugs and kisses.

Oh, how she wished Hudson was here. She desperately wanted him by her side. Wanted to share this beautiful moment with him.

"The question is, Short Stack," Robert Elliot said, "are you making sure every cowboy is pulling their weight, including you?"

Mandie laughed at her nickname and the memory of her asking Robert that same question four years ago. She hadn't heard it since Robert had moved to Montana with Rita after their wedding. She missed his pet name and their banter. Wished she had a kitchen towel to flick at him like she used to. She hiccuped a laugh and ran a knuckle under her eyes. "Yes, I'm 'pulling my weight,' Bronco Bobbie. Are you?"

"You know it." Robert jerked a finger toward the entryway. "Guess you'll have to prove it by showing us the loft a little later."

"Oh, she'll prove it, trust me," Sydney said. "Why don't we all sit down"—she gestured to the table with a bride-to-be sign on it—"and get this party started."

Robert glanced around the room. "Where's Hudson?"

Mandie's chest tightened. She didn't want to explain their situation and ruin the shower. So she simply said, "He's in Seattle."

The room grew awkward for a long, uncomfortable moment. It must have been the pitiful look on her face. *Choose happy*, she reminded herself and did her best to force her face to show it.

"We'll let you ladies have some fun," Trey said. "Us guys are going to check out some horses."

"I can't wait to see Trip." Chad's face lit up. He followed the guys outside, each one an alpha male who adored his wife and would bend over backward for her.

At three tables pulled together, Mandie took a minute to catch up with Rita, only to find out the Umatilla Native and Robert were going to have their first child. How wonderful!

"I'm thrilled your ranch is doing well," Mandie said.

She also learned Sophie's nature, wildlife, and newly added Western art had taken off in Whitefish, Montana, at Steward's Fine Art Gallery, and Chad's colt-starting business was thriving.

"She's been featured in *Cowgirl Magazine* and other prominent periodicals," Rita said as Sophie blushed.

"That is so cool." What an honor to watch the Salish-Kootenai woman flourish. Good for her. Good for them all. Watching Sydney, Rita, and Sophie survive their abusive relationships and thrive in their new lives of horses, cattle, speaking, writing, and art offered hope.

If they could have successful marriages, so could she. Right?

Mandie prayed that soon she, too, could enjoy what she loved and felt she was called to do.

And that Hudson Piccolo would be home soon.

Dressed in his favorite dark brown suit and tie, Hudson waited outside Gunner Randall's office. Loud, angry voices clashed on the other side of the door. From what he gathered, a furious woman was accusing Puget Sound Council of Environmental Attorneys of dumping pollution into local rivers and lakes.

"I'm going to take this to the media." The woman's voice gathered volume. "And you can guarantee we're going to show up Monday in protest. We'll hire our own attorneys if we have to."

"You can call the media. You can show up on Monday and protest all you want," Randall said, firing off a round of expletives. "But whomever you hire? We'll bury them in discovery and legal fees. There's no way you will ever raise enough money to come against this firm. And you know it. Trust me, we'll shut you up. No matter what it takes."

"Did you just threaten to kill me?"

Hudson had never seen this side of Randall, and he didn't like what he heard. Not one bit.

"If you don't leave right now, I'll call security and have you thrown out." More expletives exploded out of Randall.

A sharp silence cut the air. The door handle rattled, and a red-faced woman, looking to be in her late twenties, stormed out of the office and waiting room. The door slammed behind her, and she stomped down the corridor.

Seconds later, in his navy blue suit and tie and well-groomed gray hair, Randall came out all smiles but clearly flustered.

Hudson sagged in the leather chair. He wished he had stayed home. Wished he'd listened to Mandie's warnings. His gut's warnings.

"Glad you made it, son." Randall held out his hand.

Hudson sprang to his feet and shook the man's hand.

"I'm not sure what you heard in there," Randall said in a gruff tone. "We get environmentalists in here all the time, accusing the companies we represent of things that just aren't true. People like *that woman* are nothing to worry about." He seemed to school his tone. "What matters most in situations like this is keeping the partners and the investors happy."

Hudson didn't know how to respond. His parents had been upstanding attorneys and had taught him to be the same. "Yes, sir," was all he could manage.

"Let's go to dinner. I have a car waiting." Randall clapped Hudson's shoulder.

Hudson cringed at the man's touch. But he'd hear him out to see if what he'd witnessed was the morals Randall stood on or to find out if this was an isolated incident.

In the fancy restaurant in downtown Seattle where the steak and lobster were three times the cost they should be, Hudson wet his parched mouth with ice water, and Randall downed a glass of bourbon.

Hudson took a bite of buttery lobster. His mouth wanted to enjoy the seafood, but his stomach protested.

"Let's catch you up to speed on the salmon project we're working on," Randall said between bites.

Hudson wiped his mouth. "First, can we talk about what happened in your office?"

"All you need to know about that situation is that the company we represent generates millions of dollars through its investors. We don't have time for petty environmentalists. I'm sure you'll know what I mean—"

"Actually, no, I don't know what you mean. And honestly, I don't like how you treated her. And if that's how you expect me to treat people"—Hudson pushed away from the table and stood—"I'm going to have to decline this interview."

No way would he work for a man like Randall. At least his boss back home treated people with kindness and respect. And there was no way he would bring Mandie and Nona into such a toxic environment. What an idiot he'd been for even considering the job. The move. But then, maybe that's why God allowed him to come. To see how unbelievably crooked Gunner Randall was. Perhaps God wanted him to remain in Omak. Hudson could clearly see the benefits now.

He wanted to let Nona grow up in her rich culture. To learn her language. To experience their tradition together with God leading the way.

Randall leaned back in his cushy chair. "This isn't an interview, son." Randall wiped his mouth with a crisp, white linen napkin. "This is a job offer. A very lucrative one at that. I suggest you sit down, and I'll give you one more chance."

Hudson jammed his free hand in his pocket. "In all honesty, sir, I've heard enough. I'm going to have to decline your offer." Hudson tossed his napkin on the table. "Thank you for dinner."

He covered the ground at a sharp clip toward the exit. Why he'd left Mandie for something like this when he could have been helping her was beyond him. He couldn't wait to get back home. But first, he needed to clear his head and think about how he'd tell Mom the news, because to her it would be devastating, and set crisper boundaries.

Outside in the cool coastal air, he headed for the pier.

CHAPTER 12

The next day, Hudson sat at a table belonging to another high-society, fancy-wine-menu restaurant for brunch with Mom. After living in the middle of nowhere for a few years, he was no longer comfortable with suits and dresses that cost more than six months of Mandie's wages. He was eager to get back to her and Nona, especially after accidentally dropping his cell in the harbor last night when a group of rowdy college dudes reeking of beer bumped into him.

He missed calling Mandie last night. Missed her voice. Their nightly check-ins. Would she be worried? Mad? Scared? He'd have to call her as soon as he could. If he could remember her cell number. He'd have to replace all his contact info.

Awesome.

He took a sip of his stiff, black coffee and bobbed his knee, feeling like a hungry little boy about to get a severe tongue-lashing and be sent to bed with no dinner.

"I'm very sorry to hear Randall was so unprofessional." In one of her size two, lamé dresses from Switzerland, Mom sipped her mimosa. "How about I talk to him so you can have another chance at the job? Better yet, I know another law firm that's looking to hire—"

"No, Mom . . . thanks for your help, but I'm no longer a little boy. And I'm no longer a teenager. I can do this on my own."

"I'm not saying you're a child. I'm merely helping you get a better job. Is it so hard for you to accept a little assistance?" Mom eyeballed him. "God made mothers for this reason, you know." She took another sip of the bright yellow drink.

Hudson leaned forward. "Mom, I love you. You know that, right?"

"Of course you do." She gave him a motherly grin. As though she expected him to agree with her. "And I love you too."

He leaned back. "Right. So here's the deal. I don't want you to set up job interviews for me. And . . . you need to know I'm not going to move back to Seattle." His knee bobbed faster, so he crossed his ankles to get his jitters under control.

Her expression unraveled. "But, son—"

"Please don't interrupt."

She put her hands up and gave him a curt nod. Taking a long drink of her mimosa, she twirled her glass, the ice clinking off the sides.

"I'm about to marry Mandie. She's now the most important woman in my life." He waited a moment for a fiery reaction. When none came, he continued. "You're important to me, and to Mandie too. We want you in our lives. We want you to get to know Nona better."

"And I want to be in your life."

Hudson held up his hands to shush her.

"If so, you need to let us live our own lives. On the reservation." Where his dream of a lucrative job was now quashed, and, more than likely, he'd wade through a career he'd loathe for the rest of his life. Unless he could go out on his own. Or find something better. Different. But he'd be with the love of his life and her—their—precious daughter. That was the most important.

Mom's face screwed up in disapproval. "I understand. But there are no opportunities over *there* like there are here in

Seattle. You come from money. Money we worked hard for. So you could have a life—"

"Like you?" He sagged in his chair.

She downed the rest of her mimosa. "What's so bad about having a life like your father's and mine?"

"Believe it or not, I enjoy a simple life at a slower pace. Money isn't everything, Mom." Had he just quoted his fiancée? His chest lightened. He gave a slight grin and fiddled with his linen napkin.

"Next, you'll be telling me you don't want your *meager* trust fund."

"I'll save it for retirement." He uncrossed his ankles and lengthened his spine. "Better yet, I'll save it for Nona's college. And tuition for any other kids we have."

Mom's face brightened a shade or two. "You're planning on having more children?"

"As many as I can." As many as Mandie would allow. "I want to raise them in the country." He offered her an encouraging smile. "I think in time you, too, will learn to appreciate country living."

Mom scoffed. "I doubt that, though I appreciate the beauty of the land. Living there has no appeal for me. I'm a city girl through and through."

And proud of it. "But you'll come visit us, right?" He jigged his leg so hard it rattled the table.

"Occasionally. I think it would be best if you came here most of the time. There's so much more for children to do. Like the Science Center, the zoo, the aquarium, whale watching."

Enough already. He wanted to get up and leave. Go home and hold his fiancée. Kiss her senseless. "And yes, of course, we'll spend time here doing those things."

"Why don't you stay the weekend? I want to spend a little more time together before Mandie becomes 'the most important woman in your life.'"

"Mom."

"Well, it never hurts to try." Mom tossed him a wry grin. "By the way, did she like the scarf?"

"She loved it." At least he hoped so. Mom's tactless note had ruined the moment.

"Oh, good. It cost a pretty penny."

"Of course it did," Hudson mumbled. An image of the gift from Randall popped into his mind. "Hey, did you have anything to do with a basket from Gunner? I think it's strange I'd get one before being hired on to the firm."

She squirmed. "I don't know what you're talking about."

"Mom?"

"Okay. I may have suggested it. But that's it. No harm done." She waved a server over and ordered another mimosa. "When are you going home?"

"The sooner the better."

Mandie sprawled out on the wooden plank floor surrounded by unfinished silver vases and wedding favors under the bright lights of the loft. She had not heard from Hudson. Why? Was he safe? Had he been mugged? Other reasons why she didn't want to move to Seattle—her and Nona's safety.

And she'd bought him Seattle Hawks tickets for Christmas yesterday. Something she knew he loved. A special gift for helping her with the weddings.

"A Holly Jolly Christmas" played from a music app on her phone. Yeah. Not the song of her choice. She didn't even feel festive in her green-red-and-white gingerbread man sweater.

Just when she was going to change the music to country, what sounded like a stampede volleyed up the staircase and burst into the loft.

Sophie and Leena appeared, then Rita, who wore a Christmas light-up tree necklace around her neck with matching earrings. Sophie had a red bow clipped to her updo and tiny metal-decorated trees dangling from her earlobes. Laughter bubbled out of them like Christmas morning. Looking like she was feeling better, Leena wore her hair in a ponytail and sang along with the music app, her voice a bit scratchy but still lovely.

If Mandie heard "Holly Jolly" one more time, she might clobber something. She cringed and shut off the music.

"We came to help you," Sophie said. "What do you want us to do?" She glanced around the loft.

Mandie's insides swirled like a snow flurry as she attempted to pull it together. She wanted to tell them how worried she was about Hudson not calling for their nightly check-in. Too bad sharing her worries would not be professional. If only she didn't want to be alone right now. "I think Holly's family is due to arrive about noon. Can you guys help Sydney get everything ready? There's a box of Christmas decorations in the office for the rooms."

"Sure. We can do that," Rita said. "What about in here?"

"I've got this under control. Right now, this is a one-woman show." She hated to send them away. But didn't think she could hold her emotions at bay.

"When we're done with the rooms," Sophie said, "we'll come back and help you."

Mandie shook her head. "You guys are here to visit. You don't need to help me. Besides, it's just the wedding party coming minus the bride's parents. They can't head over from Spanaway until Friday."

"We don't mind." Rita fingered a star ornament. "This is beautiful, Mandie. I think you've found your calling."

"That's for sure." Sophie checked out one of the unfinished centerpieces on a nearby table. "Did you make these?"

"I sure did." Feeling encouraged, Mandie rose and joined the girls at the table. A moment later, Sydney entered the loft bundled like a snowman.

"There you are," Sydney said to Leena with a frown. Leena's face turned sullen. "You should be in bed."

Leena shrugged.

Sydney glanced around the loft. "This keeps looking better and better. I don't think anyone can top it. Well done."

She hoped Syd's compliment was confirmation that she'd get the event planning job for the guest ranch. Though Sydney had never officially given her a thumbs-up.

"And you're using the same space and decorations for your ceremony, right?" Rita asked.

Mandie shoved a fresh round of tears away. "I am. But in maroon. Not blue."

"I can't wait." Sophie gave three soft claps.

Where was Hudson? Mandie turned her head and focused on the tall corner trees so she wouldn't cry.

"I'm wondering," Sydney said, "if you ladies could help me get a handful of rooms ready."

"I can help too," Leena said to her mom.

Sydney scowled at her daughter. "You need to be in bed."

"I'm fine."

"Now, please." Sydney pointed to the exit. "At least for another day or two."

"Yes, ma'am," Leena said with a hint of sarcasm. She told everyone goodbye and dragged her feet to the stairs.

Mandie prayed Leena would be well enough to sing at least when Holly walked down the aisle. After, she'd tell her to forget about performing at her ceremony. She wanted the girl to get better and head back to college to chase her God-given gift.

"Mandie suggested we help you," Rita said. "We were about to head your way."

Mandie found the nerve to face the group and smile.

"We'll catch up with you later, Mandie." Sophie waved, and the four ladies headed toward the exit.

Not able to stand radio silence any longer, Mandie fetched her cell phone from the floor and called Hudson. Stupid voicemail.

Mandie disconnected the call and went over to Holly's to-do list.

Pick up and arrange flowers Sat and put in loft's downstairs cooler.

Check and make sure photographer's still coming.

Check on Leena. Make sure CD player is working and check sound system.

Nail down Holly's playlist. Check on Leena again.

See how menu is coming along.

"I've got to learn the correct terminology if I'm going to be an event planner," she said to the corkboard.

Mandie regarded her cell phone again. No text. No missed calls. Nothing. To fight the tears, she tapped her music app back on. "Let It Snow" blared through the speakers. She switched to country. When a love song came on, she groaned, turned off the music, and worked to the crackle of the fire.

CHAPTER 13

M andie couldn't believe she had only two days before Holly's wedding. How could it already be Friday afternoon? She prayed Holly's Vow Day would be nice and sunny, unlike today's blizzard. In the warmth of the loft and to "Silver Bells," she checked her list. Then checked it twice.

Holly's parents were to arrive by two. She needed to have a sound check with Leena, whose voice might not hold up, and run through her two songs. Maybe one. Finish the centerpieces. Have Holly approve the canned music list.

That left arranging the flowers and finishing the party favors for tomorrow, which would give her more time with Nona, who desperately needed it. Mandie's heart had sunk that morning when her daughter had clung to her leg, not wanting her to leave. Even though she had a fun playdate scheduled with Grandma Jessica. Best mom ever.

But days like this would be part of this job. Which would, yes, be hard, but it would also teach her daughter what a good work ethic, dedication, and endurance looked like. In today's world, women still had to be strong and fight for their dreams. Mandie picked up her cup and took a swig of cold coffee. Yuck. She made a face, donned her winter wear, and trudged through the storm to the lodge, blinking back the bite of snow and wind.

Inside, Holly stood by the dim fire, bawling, encircled by her bridal party. The ladies, dressed in yoga pants and sweatshirts, were doing their best to console her.

With a sickening feeling, Mandie approached them. "What's the matter?"

The bridal party turned around, and Holly lifted her quivering chin, her eyes red, tears streaking down her face. "My parents are at the airport. Their flights are canceled. Snoqualmie and Stevens passes are closed. There's no way they can get here by tomorrow." She hiccuped a sob.

"Oh dear! Um," Mandie paused, "let me see what I can do."

Holly nodded, and the bridal party went back to comforting her.

The knot forming in Mandie's belly hardened as she rushed to the ranch office. Halfway there, she stopped. If she wanted this job, she couldn't whine around to Sydney. No, she had to prove her worth. Instead, she hurried into the kitchen where the cooks were busy with lunch preparations.

"Shirley, I left my phone in the loft. Can I use yours to check the weather?"

"You sure can. It's over there on the counter." Shirley rolled out cookie dough.

At the stove, Paula stirred what smelled like a pot of beef stew. Fresh rolls stood on the counter. Mandie turned off Scotty McCreery singing "Christmas Comin' Round Again" so she could think and pulled up the weather app. The forecast specified snow all day and into the next.

"What's going on out there?" Shirley patted the dough.

"Poor Holly's frazzled. Her parents are stuck at the airport, and both passes are closed."

"Good reason to be upset." Shirley tugged a hand towel off her shoulder and wiped sweat off her face.

Think, Mandie. Holding the phone, she paced. The heels of her boots clicked on the linoleum floor. *What would Sarah Haywood do?* She tried to think like the famous decorator.

A cry came from the other room. "How can I get married without my parents?"

"Oh no." Mandie set Shirley's phone on the counter and scurried into the great room and to Holly's side. "Don't worry. We'll figure something out." She scanned the room. "Where's Nicholas?"

"I think he's still in the barn with the guys." Holly dabbed her eyes with a wadded-up tissue.

"I'll go find him if you want to go upstairs and rest."

Holly nodded and headed for the staircase over the office. The bridal party gave one another sorrowful glances and sank to the couch and chairs by the fire.

Rita and Sophie talked quietly in the gift shop. No doubt they'd caught every word. Which was fine because the ladies were prayer warriors. A few minutes later, they snuck up the stairs and into the room reserved for women in need.

The room was decorated with a Missing and Murdered Indigenous Women theme in red, white, and black colors, featuring a woman with a red handprint over her mouth on canvas. The room that saved Rita and Sophie, and so many more ladies in need. Mandie loved that room.

Outside the big bay window in the great room, snow continued to pile up. The wind picked up snowflakes, twirled them around, and slammed them to the ground.

Not knowing what to do, Mandie grabbed a cup of hot coffee and slouched in a chair at the nearest dining room table to pray. She was about to bow her head when the creak of the main lodge door opening and closing caught her attention. Seconds later, Hudson appeared, looking like a tall, buff icicle wearing a green flannel shirt, his favorite brown Stetson, and black cowboy boots. He looked hotter than she wanted him to. Way hotter.

"What are you doing here?" She didn't mean to sound so snippy. Okay, yeah, she did. Just not in front of the guests.

Hudson strode to the table and sat down beside her, his back to the bridesmaids. He gave her an apologetic look.

Mandie kept her voice low. "Why haven't you called or texted? I thought you might be hurt or something." She chewed on her bottom lip to keep from breaking down.

"Sorry I didn't call last night. My phone ended up in the harbor, thanks to a group of drunk college guys who—"

"You were down at the pier? Alone? At night?"

He tipped his head to the side. "Well, yeah. Since I was a teenager."

"That's another reason I don't want to move to the coast."

"Please hear me out."

Trembling, she nodded and wrapped her hands around her cup.

"Plus, I had trouble rebooking my flight and figured you'd be upset with me for not checking in. I wasn't able to get a new cell until I left for the airport, thanks to my mom holding me hostage at Aragosta's." He shrugged. "All the flights were booked. Thankfully, I was able to snag a ride on a buddy's private plane before everything got shut down. Listen, there's a lot to talk about. Besides, I wanted to tell you in person."

He revealed what had transpired with Gunner Randall and his decision to remain in Omak, and why.

All remnants of anger and fear dissipated like fog in warm rays of sunshine. "Thank you for choosing us. For allowing Nona to grow up here with her family and our culture." Mandie leaned across the table and gave him a sweet kiss. "I'm so glad you're okay. You had me worried."

"I'm sorry I didn't use my mom's cell to call you. I did *not* want her in our business any more than she already is."

Mandie chuckled. "I'm ashamed to admit.... I didn't call her for the same reason."

"Don't be. She's a handful."

"So, were you able to, you know, have a talk with her?"

"I sure did."

"And?"

"I'm pretty sure she's going to let us live our lives in peace."

"I hope so." Nothing would please Mandie more than to have a better relationship with her soon-to-be mother-in-law.

"I have more news."

"You do?"

Hudson was sure Mandie would be pleased. He sat back in his chair, feeling the warmth of the guest lodge. "After landing, I went to Omak to talk with my boss."

She let go of her cup and leaned forward. "Go on."

"I told him what had transpired in Seattle. We talked about how unhappy I am with my work."

"How'd he take the news?"

"He offered me a partnership."

Mandie squealed and covered her mouth as though not wanting to make a scene.

She lowered her voice. "A partnership?"

Hudson nodded. "He'd like to retire soon. Can you see how God is working this out? He closed the doors in Seattle and has opened up one heck of an opportunity here."

"I can see God at work. What'd you say?"

"Heck, yeah!"

Mandie clapped her hands. "I'm so happy for you. You've worked hard. You deserve the partnership. I'm proud of you, babe."

Hudson grabbed her hand, brushed his lips over her soft skin, and inhaled the scent of her lotion.

Mandie broke free and said, "I'm so proud of you that I have a special gift for you. I was going to give these to you for Christmas but now seems more appropriate." She pulled up the receipt on her cell and handed the phone to him.

Hudson glanced at the screen. His eyes widened. "You got me Hawks tickets?"

"I sure did."

"You know how much I love them." The Seattle SuperHawks basketball team was all he could talk about during the winter months. He knew it drove Mandie crazy.

The look on her face confirmed she'd gotten him the perfect thank-you gift. "And you can take anyone you want."

"Because you got me two of them." He held up her cell, his eyes sparkling like a child's on Christmas morning.

Hudson went to her chair, picked her up, and twirled her around. "Thank you, babe." He set her back on the floor.

"Thank you for all your help." Mandie sank to her chair. "Tell me more about the conversation with your mom."

"Like I told her, you and Nona are my priority."

"I like the sound of that."

So did he. "It felt good to stand up to her." Hudson chuckled, then grew serious. "I'm glad to be home." To support his gorgeous fiancée. "When I walked in, you looked exasperated. What's going on? Does it have anything to do with the canceled flights?"

"It does. Holly's parents are stuck at SeaTac. All the flights are canceled. The passes are closed. She's pretty upset."

"Where's the groom?"

Mandie scanned the room. "Holly thought out with the boys. They're in the barn."

"Does the groom know the wedding's off?"

Mandie shrugged. "Another good question. I'd better go find out." She released Hudson's hand and rose.

"I'll go with you." Hudson escorted Mandie to the boot-lined foyer with his hand on the small of her back. He didn't want her to tell Nicholas by herself.

After bundling up, they rushed through the blizzard and into the barn, entering through the door next to the large slider. Sure enough, the men were inside roping a dummy calf, whooping and hollering, placing bets. Some horses had their noses sticking out of the stalls, watching the hoopla.

"I didn't know Robert and Chad were coming." Hudson paused inside the barn.

"Me either. Rita and Sophie are here too."

He gestured to Robert and Chad. "Why are they here?"

"Sydney threw me a surprise bridal shower yesterday."

Great. He now felt even more stupid for leaving. Hudson shook his head. "Sorry I wasn't there to celebrate with you."

"You're here now. That's all that matters."

A slow grin spread across Robert's face when he spied Mandie. "Hey, Short Stack. Did you come for some lessons?" He winked at her before turning his attention to Hudson. "Good to see you, buddy." The men shook hands.

"No, Bronco Bobby. We did not come for lessons." Mandie gestured to the dummy calf. "You're a bronc rider. What do you know about roping?" She tossed him a playful grin before catching Nicholas's attention to pull him aside.

"I might be a bronc rider, but remember, I'm also a rancher." He swung a loop and landed the horns. Then he strutted like a rooster.

Hudson admired his skills. He took in the scene as Mandie tried to snag Nicholas Baxter's attention, but it was firmly planted on Robert and the rope. "That's right," he said to Robert. "Didn't you qualify for your first NFR this year?"

"I did."

"Right on. How'd you do?" Hudson looked at Mandie when she placed a hand on his arm and shook her head. *What?* he mouthed.

"Fifth out of fifteen. Not too shabby for my first time out." Robert coiled the rope and made a new loop.

"Not shabby at all," Hudson said. "Congrats."

"Oh my gosh," Mandie said. "Don't encourage him. We need to have his big head fit through the sliders." She finally hooked Nicholas's attention and motioned for him to meet her by the first stall.

"Very funny." Robert lifted the loop over his head, swung, and aimed at Mandie. She tried to get away. But when the lasso descended over her head, he cinched it around her waist. "Are you sure you don't want lessons?"

Mandie slipped out of the rope and flung it at him. "I'm good." Her gaze swung to Nicholas, who appeared to be enjoying the show. "Can I talk to you for a minute?"

"Sure. What's up?"

Mandie motioned to the sliding door. "Over here." She took hold of Hudson's hand and headed that way.

Hudson racked his brain, trying to find a solution. Could Holly's family travel to Oregon and up through Tri-Cities? Or up to Canada and cross the border by Oroville?

Nicholas followed them. "Is something the matter?"

Mandie told him about the canceled flights and how upset Holly was. "She's resting now."

"Oh, man. Thanks for letting me know." His face dropped. "I'll go check on her. There's no way I'm canceling this wedding."

The three of them trekked back to the lodge. Nicholas went in search of Holly. A half hour later, he slumped down the steps and joined Hudson and Mandie by the fireplace.

By the look on her face, Mandie was trying to enjoy a cup of hot cocoa and a sugary bell-shaped cookie fresh out of the oven. Hudson dunked his third cookie into a cup of coffee and shoved it into his mouth.

"How'd it go?" Mandie held the cookie on her lap.

"I talked to her parents," Nicholas said in a gloomy tone. "They went home. I got ahold of my parents. They're going to hole up in a hotel in Idaho."

"Where are they coming in from?" Hudson asked.

"Montana." Nicholas picked at the cuff of his sweatshirt.

Hudson brushed cookie crumbs off his fingers. "You're having the ceremony here to meet in the middle?"

"Yeah. Holly and her family have been here before and fell in love with the place. Since we're a ranching family, we thought it would be a good idea, even though her family is from the coast. It took a bit to convince her parents to have it here during winter. Her mom figured something like this would happen this time of year."

"I hope," Mandie said, "she didn't tell Holly 'I told you so.'"

Nicholas's neck and cheeks flamed red. "Unfortunately, she did. Holly's going to take a nap. She's exhausted." He leaned back and closed his eyes.

What a nightmare. Hudson imagined the same thing happening to him and Mandie. And it could, considering their wedding was a week away. "Since everybody's here, why don't you just wait a few days until the weather clears?"

"Because it's Christmas." Shaking her head, Mandie frowned at him. "Plus, Trey and Sydney have plans."

Nicholas let out a heavy sigh. "We're pushing things as it is, getting married here and all. On Christmas Eve. We couldn't imagine imposing on everybody's holiday."

"What about coming back and having a New Year's Eve wedding?" Hudson asked.

Nicholas's face lit up as he leaned forward. But the look on Mandie's face spelled trouble. He probably should have asked her first. Oops.

Mandie shot her fiancé a steely glare. "I—"

"We could come back in a week?" Nicholas said. "She desperately wants a December wedding."

Mandie's face paled. "I, um. I'll talk to Sydney and get back to you."

"Great. Let me know. I'll go tell Holly." Nicholas rushed up the stairs.

Mandie turned to Hudson. "What were you thinking?" Her voice cracked as she set her cookie on the coffee table. "That's *our* wedding day."

Hudson blinked at her for several seconds. In a calm lawyer tone, he said, "I was thinking maybe we could swap. We could have ours on Saturday, and they could come back in a week. Your family's already here. The only person in my family is my mom."

"What about your friends?"

"I've been on the rez for three years now. My friends are here."

Mandie twisted her engagement ring around her finger. "I don't know if Sydney will agree with the swap." Her voice shifted to a tone that made his gut flip. "You cannot go around offering alternatives without checking with me first. I'm the wedding planner, not you."

"We'll figure something out." When Mandie's countenance did not soften, he went into defense mode. Hudson gestured to the staircase Nicholas had climbed. "I couldn't let them down."

"Was it your job to make the call?"

"Probably not." How could he fix this?

She inhaled and let out her breath. Examined him for a long moment. "I appreciate your willingness to help. But, babe, I wish you would have talked to me before suggesting a solution."

CHAPTER 14

Mandie and Holly sat at a table in the soft blue glow of the light in the loft. Saturday at ten in the morning, snow continued to pile higher and higher. The passes were still closed, and the airplanes were still grounded. The hopelessness in Holly's eyes made Mandie cave.

"Are you sure we can come back for a New Year's Eve wedding?" Holly's eyes had sprung to life when Mandie had made the offer minutes ago. She looked adorable in her pink sweater and skinny jeans with a hint of mulberry on her lips. The offer only added to her vibrancy.

"I'm positive." Being professional and all, Mandie stuck on a cheerful face. Holly's shift from tears to delight made it easier to feign joy.

"This is everything I've ever wanted. And New Year's Eve is still in December. You making my dream come true, well, I can't thank you enough. Like I said before, I'm going to tell all my friends how amazing you and this guest ranch are."

Wow. How sweet. "I'm glad you like it. Any and all referrals are appreciated."

"Will the flowers stay fresh for a week or will they wilt?"

"In all honesty, I'm not certain. But considering yours are roses and carnations, I think there's a good chance they'll be presentable."

"And if not?"

"I called local florists to see what they have available. I think we'll be able to replace them. But it will cost you more money."

"I understand. Please keep me posted." Holly rose and made a sweep around the room. She touched the ornaments, wiped her eyes, brushed her fingers over the frosted tree boughs, and ambled back to the table. "The roads are supposed to be clear tomorrow. We'll head back to the west side and see you next Friday."

Mandie stood and gave her a comforting hug. "See you next Friday."

She slouched in her seat as Holly made her way to the exit and down the stairs. In all honesty, she didn't want to give up her wedding day. She liked things the way they were. Liked the original plan. But the joy on Holly's face was worth it.

She'd have her wedding. Someday. Maybe Hudson was right. A Valentine's ceremony might be nice.

Footsteps stomped up the stairs, and Hudson appeared looking rather gloomy.

"Are you still mad at me?" He took a cautious step toward her.

"A little." Disappointed was more like it.

He took two more steps. "Do you still love me?" He gave her an adorable, sappy look.

In return, she gave him a forgiving grin. "Of course."

"Do you still want to marry me?" A few more steps.

"I do." She liked the sound of those two sweet words. A lot. She opened her arms for a hug.

Hudson strode the few remaining steps and embraced her. "I'm sorry I made a mess of things."

"It's okay. Holly's thrilled. That's what matters most." Mandie took a seat and slouched.

He settled in a chair next to her. "Let's get through Christmas, then figure this out. I'm sure we can still have our wedding sometime next week if you still want a December one."

"It's okay." Mandie gave him her best smile, trying to remain positive and professional. "Like you said, we'll figure something out."

"You decide what you want to do and let me know. In the meantime, I'm going to pick up Nona from your sister and take her for a tea party at the Dam."

"Thanks for taking her today." Mandie took in the room. "The good news is, we can keep everything up for the week. We'll just have to dust and sweep and stuff Thursday."

"I'll have the week off and will do whatever you want me to."

"Thanks. And thank you for taking Nona today. She's going to love the tea party."

Hudson leaned over and kissed her. "I'll see you later." He palmed her shoulder. "By the way, don't bother cooking dinner. I've got it covered. I'll meet you at your house about six."

Mandie nodded. "Sounds good to me." Until then, she planned to go home, soak in a hot tub with a carton of chocolate-and-caramel ice cream and a cinnamon-scented candle, and put on Christmas music.

Because she had to trust that God would work everything out for their good. Or she'd unravel.

After the successful tea party, Hudson dropped Nona off with Mandie's older sister, Marlee. In the driveway of her house in Elmer City, he texted Sydney.

Is the coast clear?

Sydney: *Clear as a summer day.*

Hudson: *On my way.*

He drove back to the loft, planning to make things right with Mandie. He could never figure out why she wanted a New Year's Eve wedding when Christmas was her favorite holiday of the year.

Fifteen minutes later, he parked near the hay barn and rushed up the stairs to the loft. Mandie's mom, Jessica; Sydney; Rita; Sunny, Mandie's younger sister; and Sophie were busy spreading white flowers across two of the tables. A few minutes later, Shirley joined them with snacks and two thermoses of coffee.

He dug into a decorated wreath-shaped sugar cookie and poured a cup of steamy brew.

"Thanks for staying," Hudson said to Shirley.

"I wouldn't miss this for anything." She patted his arm. "I'll leave Sunday instead of today. It's all good."

Hudson hugged her then turned to the ladies. "Okay, what's the plan?"

"First of all," Jessica said as she set a hand on her hip. "When Mandie was a little girl, all she talked about was having a Christmas Eve wedding."

I knew it. Hudson chuckled.

"Until her then BFF had hers on the same day," Sunny said. "All a sudden, Mandie claimed she wanted a New Year's Eve wedding. What a crock of horse poo."

"That makes me feel a whole lot better," Hudson said. "But the question is, how are we going to get her here tomorrow?"

"Don't worry about it," Sydney said with a sassy smile. "I'll be talking to her about event planning. I've already texted her. We have an appointment at two." Sydney got up and brought Mandie's storyboard and to-do list closer.

"She has everything lined out," Rita said.

Sydney tapped the board. "All we have to do is follow her lists."

Sophie nodded. "And check them twice."

Everyone laughed and agreed that Mandie had OCD issues.

"I have the cake done," Shirley said. "All I have to do is frost it and add maroon flowers."

"You ladies are amazing." He choked up. "Thanks for making Mandie's dreams come true."

"My girl deserves it." Moisture pooled in Jessica's eyes.

"Yes, she does." Sydney turned to the storyboard. "We have to change out the party favors. Add maroon flowers to the centerpieces and the trees." She smiled at every person in the room as she spoke. "I talked to the florist in Omak. She's going to hook us up with fresh and silk flowers. I don't know which kind yet. But she says she has connections and can make it happen. So I'm going to trust her."

Hudson picked up one of the party favor snow globes meant for Holly's wedding. "What are our party favors?"

Sydney gestured to the list. "According to this, they're done. We simply have to locate them. To answer your question, I honestly don't know what they are. But—"

Sunny raised a finger. "I think I know where they are."

"Where?" Hudson and Jessica asked in unison.

"In the closet in the gift shop."

"In *my* gift shop?" Sydney palmed her chest. "How did I miss them?"

Sunny swung her gaze to her mom. "She said something about having a surprise in there. It's the only thing that I can think of. What other surprise would it be?"

"Bridesmaids' gifts?" Jessica glanced at the others and shrugged.

"I didn't think of that." Sunny scrunched her nose and mouth.

"I'll check after a bit," Sydney said. "For now, let's get to work. We don't have much time."

Everyone started to swap out flowers when Hudson said, "What about her dress? What about Nona's dress? The music? The food?" An unexpected sense of panic surged through him, causing him to break out in a sweat.

"That's all taken care of." Jessica picked up a silver vase and inspected it.

Hudson wiped his forehead with the sleeve of his green Western shirt. "What about all the blue lights? Do they even go with maroon?"

Jessica faced Hudson. With a voice that would gentle any wild Mustang, she said, "What you need to do, son, is calm down and call your best man and your groomsmen and let them know that there's been a change in plans. Are your outfits ready?"

"I have no idea." Hudson looked forward to wearing new jeans, shirts, vests, cowboy boots, and matching black Stetsons. When Jessica frowned at him, he grinned and added, "You know, she's always wanted to marry a cowboy. So we're making that happen."

"And that's why we love you." After Jessica set the vase down, she strode over to Hudson and gave him a big hug. She teared up and cupped his face. "Thank you for loving my daughter like you do. She's fortunate to have you. Mistakes and all." She rose onto her tiptoes, planted a motherly kiss on the side of his face, and patted his cheek.

Hudson swallowed hard. "I'm the blessed one, Mom."

Calling her mom opened the floodgates. He gave her another hug before she went back to her spot at the table, sniffing and fanning her face.

"So," Hudson said. "I'm going to trust that one of you has called the pastor."

The ladies stopped and looked at one another. Each of them shook their heads and giggled.

Hudson groaned. "I'll make the call."

"Another reason we love you." Sydney winked at him, and the others concurred.

All they had to do now was make sure Mandie showed up for her own wedding.

CHAPTER 15

In the ranch office and across the coffee table from Sydney, Mandie fidgeted on the sofa. She wished she knew why her boss had called her in. Was she wrong to have offered Holly another day without clearing it with Sydney first?

Her attention flicked from Glenda, who was busy on the computer, to the Seven Tine Guest Ranch manifesto hanging on the wall to her right. *Honesty and Integrity are the Seven Tine's Foundation.* Had she not led with integrity? *Lead by Example.* She tried to be an example of grace and was accommodating. *Respect and Enjoy Each Other and the Land We Live On.* Had she disrespected Sydney by not clearing the date change?

Mandie crossed her arms and pressed them against her churning belly. Then went back to the manifesto.

Make Goals and Prepare for the Ruts in the Road. This had definitely been a rocky path. *Stand on Your Word.* She had done her best, hadn't she? *Make Sure Every Horse, Cow, and Cowboy Pull Their Weight.* A memory of her and Robert's playful banter swept into her mind. She smiled at the memories.

Was this even about the job? Was it about Leena? She hated it when her thoughts ran rampant.

Sydney ambled into the office, nibbling on a cracker with one hand, the long package of more in the other. "I was never this sick with Lester."

How was she going to tell Nona her wedding was postponed? Her daughter was so excited for the New Year's Eve wedding.

"The reason I called you in today was to talk to you about Holly's wedding."

Okay, so it was about the job. Mandie rested her hands in her lap. "I'm sorry I changed her date without asking you."

"Oh, that's not an issue."

It's not?

Sydney took another bite of cracker and set the rest on the coffee table by an unfinished 7Up.

Mandie's tummy continued to twist and twirl. She desperately wanted to be the ranch's event planner. Especially now that Hudson had declined the Seattle job. She was here to stay. With Nona and her amazing husband-to-be.

"There's been a lot of hiccups this month, hasn't there?"

"You can say that again." *But no need to.*

"How do you think you've handled everything?"

Me? The question caught Mandie off guard. She remained poised. Professional, even though they'd been friends for some time now and Sydney had treated her more like a sister than an employee. She unfolded her arms, set her clammy hands in her lap, and sat up straighter. "Well, I tried to keep everything organized and on track. When problems arose, I tried to find suitable solutions."

"That's right. You've worked hard all month. And what you did was create the exact vision of a bride's dream. Her Winter Wonderland." Sydney studied Mandie with an encouraging look. "You managed to envision every single tiny detail. You organized everything from fifteen trees to delicate snow globes with a special touch of Mandie. Best of all, you chose to give up your wedding day so another bride could have her December happily ever after."

"What are you saying?" Mandie chewed her bottom lip.

"I think, because of your hard work, dedication, willingness to endure, and selflessness, there are two things you get to have today." Sydney took a sip of her soda.

Huh? Two things? What was Sydney talking about? "Which are?"

"The title of Seven Tine Guest Ranch Event Planner." Sydney finished the cracker and wiped her hand on her maternity jeans.

Warmth radiating in her chest, Mandie clasped her hands. "Wow, I . . ."

"I know, wild, huh?" Sydney gave her a sweet laugh. "The second thing you get today is your very own Christmas Eve Vow Day."

A Christmas Eve Vow Day? Her face flushed, and her heartbeat pounded in her ears. "What are you talking about, Sydney?" The threat of tears stung her eyes. She felt like she was sitting on a galloping horse with no reins—totally out of control. "Hudson and I haven't discussed it. Nothing's ready. His mom's not here. Nobody is. What about my flowers? The pastor?" She wanted to feel joy, thankful even, but fear pressed on her chest like a 750-pound bale of hay.

Sydney held up her palm to stop Mandie from babbling on. "A little birdie told me, and a few others, that your childhood dream was not a New Year's Eve wedding, but it was indeed a Christmas Eve wedding. And so, you have one hour to get yourself ready to meet the cowboy of your dreams in the loft to profess your love and commitment in front of God and all of us who love you more than you'll ever know. And by the way, his mom is here."

She is? "But . . . I don't understand."

Sydney reached for another cracker. "What don't you understand?" She took a nibble.

"Who set this up? Who took care of all the arrangements?"

"Besides you and your lists and storyboard?" Sydney took another sip of soda. "Hudson, for starters. This was all his idea. Poor guy feels so bad about not calling you while in Seattle and for offering Holly your wedding date, he's willing to do anything to give you your December wedding." Sydney's eyes sparkled. "Besides, we all pitched in because you have done so much for all of us over the years. You've sacrificed so much for your daughter, we all wanted to do something special for you. This is how much we love and appreciate and value and believe in you, sweet friend."

"I . . . I don't know what to say."

"How about 'Thanks, boss?'" Glenda gave her a smile and a wink. "Well done, by the way." She went back to clicking her fingers across the computer keyboard.

Mandie hated how flustered she was. She shifted her position. "Yes . . . um, you're right. Thanks, Syd."

"You're welcome. Now . . . how about you go get ready in the Hummingbird room and say 'I do' in exactly one hour." Sydney checked her watch. "That's now fifty minutes. You better skedaddle."

Mandie jumped to her feet, raced around the end of the coffee table, and embraced the best boss and friend she could ever have.

In the Hummingbird room, Jessica stood by the window holding up Mandie's chiffon-and-lace wedding gown. Mandie rushed over to her and gave her a big squeeze.

"Thank you, Mom. I love you so much."

"I love you, too, honey." Jessica patted her back. "You'd better get ready. There's a handsome cowboy waiting for you in the loft."

Mandie released her mom. "Handsome is right. I can't wait to see him."

Out the window, Parker and Tucker were hitching Chokecherry and Myrrh, who had recovered and was now in good health, to the sleigh. There were already a few cars parked beside the hay barn. Too bad she hadn't caught a glimpse of Hudson.

"You have an amazing man who's going to take care of you and stick by your side."

"I do." Again, Mandie giggled at the two powerful words. The two words that would seal their love. "That sounded good." She took her dress from Jessica and slipped into the bathroom to prepare for one of the best days ever.

Five minutes later, Mandie came out in her soft, flowing gown that made her feel like a princess. "What about the food?"

Jessica caught her breath and pressed a hand to her neck. "You are beautiful." She knuckled tears away from under her eyes and found her voice. "Food is taken care of." She handed Mandie thick wool socks and white cowgirl boots, then plucked a tissue from a box on the nightstand.

Mandie gathered the dress and eased to the edge of the bed. She pulled on the socks. "What about our pastor?"

Jessica checked her watch. "He'll be here in fifteen."

"We didn't have rehearsal."

"You know what to do."

"Sydney said Lauren made it?"

"She flew in this morning on someone's highfalutin jet. Trey picked her up at the airport so she wouldn't have to traverse the roads in the snow."

"What about the flowers?" Mandie rose to her feet and smoothed her dress.

"Sydney has a friend with a friend."

"What about—"

"Mandie!" Jessica crossed the room and held her daughter's shoulders. "You need to let go and let God. Especially if you're going to be an event planner."

Mandie relaxed her tense muscles. "You're right; I am. Because I got the job!"

"That's wonderful," Jessica said. "I'm proud of you, honey."

Mandie hugged her mom, stepped back, and put up a finger. "What about my hair and makeup?"

Mom craned her neck and gazed at the door. "Come on in, girls."

Marlee and Sunny bounded into the room, holding up Mandie's makeup case, a curling iron, hairspray, combs, and hairpins.

"Let's get to work." Marlee held up the makeup case and flashed her sister a feisty smile. "We've got a lot of work to do."

At three o'clock sharp, Mandie stood at the base of the dim staircase with her arm hooked around Jessica's. When Leena started singing "Yours" by Russell Dickerson, they ascended the luminary-clad steps. And when they crested the staircase, Mandie gasped.

Maroon had infused Holly's Winter Wonderland. Leena's angelic voice floated through the air. Blue lights glowed perfectly with the other wedding hues, as did the roaring woodstove. Her family and friends stood as Lester and Nona made their way down the aisle. One looked like a little cowpoke, matching the groomsmen, and the other, a dainty princess in her silky maroon gown, matching floral hairpiece, and tiny white cowgirl boots.

Thank you, Lord, for this man, his devotion, and Your favor and blessings. From here on out, you've got the reins.

With that, she stepped toward the rest of her life. Toward the one man she could count on to love her. To be her partner and stick by her side. Looking handsome in his jeans, white shirt, maroon vest, black boots and Stetson, and rose boutonniere, Hudson stood at the end of the loft, in front of an arch covered in flowers, beaming, tears shimmering in his eyes.

What more could she ask for?

Hudson blinked away the moisture blurring his vision. He couldn't get over how beautiful his bride looked in her white, lacey dress with white fur wrapped around her shoulders. The gleam in her brown eyes was clearly visible through the veil covering her gorgeous face.

The closer she got, the faster his heart beat. All he wanted to do was wrap her in his arms and promise to never let go. By the time she reached her spot beside him, her beauty about unraveled his self-control. After she handed her bouquet off to Marlee, he took her hands in his and mouthed, "Love you."

She mouthed back, "Love you more."

"Love you most." He squeezed her hands.

The pastor smiled. "Dearly beloved . . ."

"You may kiss the bride." The pastor smiled at Mandie and nodded at Hudson.

With gentle passion, Mandie's husband captured her mouth with what felt like a committed promise to love and protect her and to raise Nona as his own. To take care of them for the rest of their lives. To become one under God.

She returned the kiss with a vow to love and honor her cowboy. To support his new partnership and honor his willingness to remain on the reservation. And to finally trust God. Completely. After all, He'd blessed her well beyond her wildest dreams.

With God, all things are possible.

A NOTE FROM THE AUTHOR

T hank you for reading Mandie and Hudson's story. They truly are a gift to each other.

I'm thrilled that a reader friend, Bobbi Jean Bell, suggested Mandie have her story told. Not only to find out if she found a man who would stick by her side, and for Nona to have a daddy, but also because I needed to write a story where Sydney, Rita, and Sophie could be seen with men who treated them with respect and love, unlike their abusive exes.

After years of writing the Seven Tine Guest Ranch Romance series and crying over the loss of my niece to domestic violence, I had to write a story with joy, forgiveness, hope, and laughter.

To find out more about domestic violence and abuse, go to https://carmenpeone.com/resources/.

To learn more about the Seven Tine Ranch Romance series, go to https://carmenpeone.com/.

You can sign up for my newsletter and be the first to hear about new Carmen Peone books and deals at https://carmenpeone.com/connect/.

You can also join "The Roundup," my Facebook author group, where we talk about Carmen Peone books, name characters, enter giveaways, and swap stories. Join here: https://www.facebook.com/groups/970868327642674.

ACKNOWLEDGMENTS

Thanks to my first readers Elizabeth Braaten, Sara Turnquist, Heidi Thomas, and Kathy Anderson for your loving and honest feedback. I'm thankful for writer friends like you!

To my editor Susan Cornell, once again you made my story shine. Thank you for your amazing suggestions.

To Shane Coleman, Utah financial attorney, for being my seatmate on the flight from Utah to Spokane and for answering my questions concerning types of attorneys and their lifestyles. I love when God shows up and plops someone right beside me exactly when I need them.

Thanks to Alice Trego for suggesting the name Myrrh; Sylvia Jane Peasley, Colville tribal member, for suggesting the name Chokecherry, or Timpts in Nez Perce; Dianne Bohnet Dust for suggesting the name Parker; Sarah Taylor for suggesting the name Tucker; Toni Brenton Thompson for suggesting the name Jessica; Georgia Davenport for suggesting the name Sunny; and Jennifer Jones Wood for suggesting the name Marlee.

All of these ladies are in my Facebook group, *The Roundup*, where we have fun talking about Carmen Peone books, naming characters, and swapping stories.

ABOUT THE AUTHOR

Award-winning author Carmen Peone lives with her tribal husband, Joe, on the Colville Confederated Indian Reservation in Northeast Washington. She gathered cultural knowledge from family and elders and studied the language and various cultural traditions and legends under the late Marguerite Ensminger. She is a horse and photography enthusiast.

With a degree in abnormal psychology, the thought of writing never entered her mind, until she married her husband, and they moved to the reservation after college. She came to love the people and their heritage, desires to create a legacy for her family, and loves to write inspirational stories of hope, healing, and horses that lead to happily ever after.

Carmen loves to hear from readers. Connect with her online: https://carmenpeone.com/